Souls of Truett Lane

KC McGee

Souls of Truett Lane

ISBN 978-09998931-3-5

This is a work of fiction. Names, characters, places, and incidents either are the product of the Author's imagination or are used fictitiously. Any resemblance to actual persons living or dead, business establishments, events or locales is entirely coincidental. The publisher does not have any control over and does not assume any responsibility for author or third -party websites or their content.

Pengate Publishing

www.pengatepublishing.org

Printed in the United States of America

They Will All Come

The neighbors stood on the street in front of William's house, everyone was crying, hugging one another saying their good-byes to the family. It was always so hard being a military family, you just never get to stay in one place long enough. It gets harder and harder for everyone especially when you're growing up moving and leaving friends. Sabien and his family watched as they drove off waving until they could no longer see them. It was a very tough day watching them pack up to leave. They all went inside their houses Sabien went to his room once he was in the house, he did not want to talk to anyone. The sadness of not seeing his friend anymore had taken a toll on his spirit, he just wanted to be left alone. His sister sat on the couch watching television, his mom went back into the kitchen, this would be the saddest day for him he thought, as he lay his head on his pillow. William cried all the way to the airport, his mother looked back at him, "Son you will be okay, where we're going, you'll make plenty of new friends" she told him wiping his eyes.

William thought of all the times he and Sabien played ball in the street in front of the house for hours. "I don't think I want new friends." He said to his mom turning from the window. "Oh no." She answered. "Well, we'll see how you feel once we're in our new place in sunny California!" She said looking from her window as they pulled into the airport.

"Here we go." His dad says loudly opening the door of the car. They all stood at the trunk grabbing their bags to check because they had to go through security. William grabbed the hand drum from his pants placing it into his carry-on bag while no one was watching. "Dad I want to stay." William tells his father holding his hand as he pulls his bag toward the walkway of the airport. When they got on the plane William took the window seat. "Go on son it'll be a long ride." His father said to him as he sat down. William was incredibly sad, the stewardess kept coming over asking William if he was okay, they even gave him ice cream. William looked out the window until he fell off to sleep. When he woke up, they were in California, everyone on the plane was standing up around him grabbing their bags lining up to walk off the plane. The pilot stood at the doorway of the plane shaking everyone's hand along with the stewardess, they welcomed everyone to California. Once they were out of the airport his father rented a car to get them to their new home in military housing. It was a long ride. William had thought of the first time he met Sabien and how he thought he was funny looking. He wore a mohawk and always carried around toy soldiers in his hand making them fight all the time. He did not believe he would ever find a friend like him ever again. Once they reached the corner to drive onto Truett Lane William sighed loudly they had really moved. What would he do for friends now? He thought as his father parked in the driveway. The movers would not be there for another couple of days. It was a big empty house with five bedrooms.

His parents went around the house checking everything, the water faucets, gas pipes, and all the bathrooms. It was a two-story house all and of the bedrooms were upstairs. They went upstairs to check them out. "Come on William grab your bag, let's go check out your new bedroom you don't have to share with your brother anymore you have your own." His father told him toting his bag over his shoulder heading up to the room. It was a long hallway with rooms on each side of the wall. William ran to the one room directly ahead of him near the bathroom, it faced the master bedroom where his parents would sleep. It was also one of the bigger rooms in the house. "Dad I want this one," he said taking a spin around the room throwing his bag down into the corner of the room. "Aha something to smile about, honey I think I found something he likes!" His father yelled out to William's mother. "Okay son this will be your room for now enjoy," His father said taking his bag down the hallway. William's brother was running around the house making so much noise, he also had a young little sister who couldn't walk yet. William's grandmother had brought them over before they got to California. His father's parents had been in California for some time they loved it there. They would come to visit every now and then but not much. The flight from New York was so long. Once the evening came the grandparents, left but they brought over air mattresses, blankets, and food for the family to eat until the movers came. William's father helped him set his air mattress up in his room. William wanted it to be near the wall where he could look out of the window at night. When it was time for bed the house grew quiet. William put his pajama's on and sat on his mattress. He pulled his bag over to the edge of the mattress. He laid in bed put the covers on staring out at the window. He really missed home, this place wasn't home to him he was very sad. He turned over to the wall thinking of all his friends back in New York, boy was he going to miss them. He remembered the hand drum, turning to his other side, he grabbed onto his bag ravaging through it looking for his hand drum, when he got it, he turned over onto his back staring up at the ceiling.

He began to shake the hand drum from side to side as he fell off to sleep. While he shook it something was happening all around him outside of his new home in California, the spirits of the native Americans who'd died started to come up from the ground all around the housing complex, most of them walking toward William's new home. Some were native Americans, and some were American cowboys. All the while William and his family slept.

Sabien was never to take anything from the reservation without permission and he would never tell William the story of how he gifted it to him or how his friend's world would forever change after receiving it. Sabien was born of two very tribal Indigenous parents who were both members of a tribe very close to the base where they lived. His mother and father both practiced and celebrated all tribal traditions, he visited his grandparents there all the time. The morning before William and his family was to leave Sabien's mother took him and his siblings up to the reservation to check on the elders of the tribe. Sabien's mother and father were both medical doctors in the US Navy they joined to learn the practices of Americans to assure themselves that they would be knowledgeable on and off the reservation, they never stop practicing there learned tribal experiences and would make sure that Sabien and his siblings would do the same. That day when they made it onto the reservation Sabien's mother walked off to the houses, she always went to the grandparent's house first before seeing any of the others. She would go from door to door checking up on them. When Sabien thought that she was too busy to notice him walking away he began to run toward the wooded area in the back of the homes. He could hear drums beating loudly as he walked through the bushes and the leaves and fallen branches would crack underneath his feet. As he followed the sound of the drum, it got louder as he grew closer, the trees whistled around him. When he reached the area where the drumming was coming from, he began to creep into the bushes grabbing them away from his face to peek in. What he saw would intrigue him to want to take something to give to William, he knew it would be special. He dazed off watching the tribal men dance around the dirt, holding small hand drums as fire shot out from the colored rocks as they danced. Grandpa would bellow out a song followed by chants, guiding the spirit, his grandpa would call it. The rock in the middle of the circle where grandpa stood would be the most beautiful of them all. As fire burned from it, the rock would light up blue and white, the flames would go high and low with every chant. It was mesmerizing, Sabien stood back watching in silence. When grandpa would finish his chant and song the other tribal men would continue dancing shaking the drum, the fire on their rocks would flare up and down as if it was dancing along with them. Grandpa screamed out one last chant taking a stick from the side of the rock placing it over the fire holding it to the sunset skies, then bringing it to his mouth, blowing it out. When he blew it out, all the fire from each of the rocks went out leaving smoke, the smoke still moving as if it was still dancing to the sound of the drum. Sabien watched in awe while grandpa went over to each of the tribal men blowing smoke from his mouth into their faces. They would place the drum down onto the rock when he was done, walking off into the bush. Sabien watched until he saw the back of grandpa's feathered helmet leaving through the bush before going over to the middle rock searching it over to see where or how it had fire, he moved quickly as he didn't want anyone to know he was there. He scanned the area of drums thinking which one of them would be easiest to take and would go unnoticed if someone came in after him, laying his eyes on the drum closet to the entrance of the woods he began to go for it when he heard the rustling of the leaves, he looked up to see the trees and bushes shaking like someone was coming through. He ran over toward the drum grabbing it keeping his head down as he heard someone calling out to him. "Hey, what are you doing!" The man yelled rushing after Sabien. He sprinted toward the bushes jumping in, running as fast as his legs could carry him. He ran so fast he could hear the whistling of the air in his ears. He kept his head forward so that he wouldn't be recognized. Placing the drum into his pants, he used his hands to clear each bush as he ran through them. When he reached the edge of the wooded area where the opening was to enter the houses he stopped, putting his head to his knees panting heavily to catch his breath. He reached down to check to make sure the drum was there. He hurried as he could hear the man's feet trampling over the crackling leaves of the woods to catch him. He headed toward his grandparents' house to meet his mother hoping she'd be ready to go. He walked quickly brushing himself off looking straight ahead he was caught off guard by the tapping on his shoulder from his grandpa. "Sabien where have you been?" He asked him, smiling. "We've been waiting for you son." I um…I was in…" "Oh too busy getting into trouble to spend a little time with old grandpa?" "No grandpa I was actually looking for you." He said to him. "Hahaha!" Grandpa laughed, "Looking for me son? I was calling out to the spirits of your ancestors hoping they'd come to heal us poor souls." He told him grabbing his hand. "Come son lets go find your mommy." Sabien began to walk with his grandpa looking over his shoulder, hoping no one else catches him off guard as they walked along the hill toward the houses. Grandpa put his hands to his back, still wearing his tribal gear, his feathered skirt moved slowly with his hips. "So, I hear your friend is leaving you son?" He says to Sabien, "Yes." Sabien said shaking his head. "Yeah, that's always hard for you I know especially now that you're older, but you know good friends never leave you." he tells him pointing to his shoulder. "If you love him, you'll always be connected spiritually, here son." He said grabbing two feathers from his head, then taking a rock from his small pocket sown into his skirt. "You take this and give it to your good friend as a parting gift, tell him whenever he begins to miss you, if he holds this rock in his hand tightly the spirits will let you know he needs you." He tells him as they approach the car where his mother was standing with his siblings waiting. "Here we are son, your mother, she's dedicated to serving in a place that never served her back, the choices they make." He said, rolling his eyes hugging Sabien. "Until next time son." He tapped Sabien on his chest and waved. "Bye grandpa!" he said getting into the car. As he shut the door, he noticed a man standing on the edge of the driveway staring at him. He nodded his head and winked at him with a smirk. Sabien quickly turned his head and felt in his pants for the drum. He sighed, it's there, he thought to himself looking at the man as they drove by. The man watched closely saying to him. "See you soon," with his lips to Sabien as they drove past him. Sabien leaned back into his seat. Once they were home Sabien and his siblings ran from the car, everyone was out saying their goodbyes to William and his family. Sabien rushed over to the stairwell of his house to place the gifts grandpa had given him near the door. He covered them with the newspaper to be safe until he came back. He scurried off toward the kids in the middle of the cul-de-sac yelling out loudly, "Hide and Seek Everyone! I'm counting!" He ran toward the trees near the play area near the side lawn and began to count. He saw William coming up on the side of him before he put his head to his arm. He nodded at him and pointed for him to hide over behind the building where no one ever goes to look. When he was done counting, he went over meet him to give him the drum, he ran as fast as he could so that no one would follow him looking all around the building. William was nowhere to be found, he started to get worried that he didn't get his crypted message across when he was snatch into a crease in the walls between the houses. "Shh!" William said to him. "What did you want?" He asked. Sabien reached into his pants. "Whoa what are you doing?" William said turning away. "Man no, Sabien said. "Here I brought you something back to take with you." He handed William the drum. "Wow! This is cool" beginning to shake it Sabien grabbed his hand. "No don't shake it out here, put it away you can't let anyone know I gave it to you not anyone, you only shake it in private when you want to hear from me the spirits will let me know." He tells him. "Spirits?" He questioned. "Yes, they will call out to me just watch and see." They could hear the other children calling out that they'd been spotted. William put the drum into his front pocket and covered it with his shirt, leaning in to give Sabien a fist bump. "We are friends forever man, I will never forget you," he tells him holding back tears. "You're my best friend, remember shake the drum when you think of me," he tells him. Another fist bump and they ran out yelling trying to make it to the tree to be safe.

What We Don't Know Won't Hurt Us

When the family woke up the next morning everything around them seemed to be out of place. William could hear his mother coming down the hallway to wake him, he jumped to his feet looking all around in his covers looking for the hand drum. He had to hide it before his mom would enter the room. He was in a panic standing to his feet shaking out the blanket he had over him that night moving the floor mattress all around. It was nowhere to be found. He went over to his backpack shook it out flinging his clothes all over the room then to his other bag snatching things out as fast as he could to find it, but soon the door started to creek open. "William honey are you up?" His mom asked in a whisper. "I am mom, I'm up." William answered back. "Is it okay to come in son?" She said standing with the door cracked open, "Are you decent?" She asked him, "Oh mom please give me a few minutes, I will be down." "Okay son, just brush your teeth and wash your face I'm going to get your siblings up, see you soon son". William scurried around the room turning over every piece of clothing that he'd thrown around. He was frantic. Where could the hand drum be? He thought after getting exhausted from looking, he sat on his mattress holding his hands to his head thinking, where could it be?

He was so upset at the fact that he couldn't find it, he gave up, grabbed his toothpaste and toothbrush and ran to the bathroom. While brushing his teeth he could hear his mom in the room getting his siblings together for breakfast. While brushing his teeth he thought about the hand drum, as he went down to spit the toothpaste out, he covered his face in water. He heard the hand drum shaking, he dried his face ran into his room looking around the room for it once again, until his mom screamed his name. He took off his pj's and changed into a shirt and jeans.

He ran to the hallway. "Yes, mom I'm coming." When he walked away from his room, he heard the hand drum once again, it sounded as if it was coming from downstairs. William rushed to the stairs to meet his mother and his siblings. "Good morning." His siblings said to him smiling. "Hello." William said to them running past them to get to the bottom of the stairs. He was listening for the hand drum. When they all got downstairs and into the kitchen, they were startled to see that all the windows and all the cabinets even the back door, the front door, every door in the house was open. His mom stood looking around the house holding onto her baby girl and holding his little brother by the shoulder. "No one move," she said walking them toward the front door peeking out. "Son!" She called out to William. "You stand here in the doorway while I look around the house, don't move or come back inside until I say so." She put her hands out. "Stay here." She said creeping away she was so nervous, what could have happened? Why were all the windows and doors and cabinets open in the house? It was as if before his dad had left for work, he opened everything up, and she knew that it wasn't at all possible that he did it because she woke up to make him breakfast at 5am and walked him out locking up the house behind him. She was ultimately baffled. She came back to the children, stood outside with them and looked around the neighborhood to see if there were any suspicious characters hanging around only to see that a lot of the other neighbors were standing outside looking around their houses, and talking to one another about the same thing. They too had the same thing happen in their house, the windows and cabinets and doors were open all over the house. She grabbed the children closing her robe tying it around her waist walking toward the mailboxes where some of the neighbors were standing talking. "Hi, I'm Sara your new neighbor." She said introducing herself holding out her hand for handshakes. "I overheard you all talking about the windows and doors and cabinets, is this something that happens often here? I was startled when I woke up this morning, my husband left earlier, I don't know what's going on." She said frantically. "Hi, I'm Barbra Bennett." "I'm Sasha Marshall." "I'm Joy Roberts." They all introduced themselves. Barbra began to explain shaking her head. "No this has never happened, we think there may have been a small trimmer, or earthquake of some kind we were all discussing going in to watch the news except we're all a little afraid to go back in." She said looking over at her house where the door was wide open. "So where are you from?" Sasha asked. "We are both from Canada, but we have been stationed in upstate New York for the last 3 years." His mom told them. "Oh, nice so Canada huh you're a very long way from home," Joy said. "And who do we have here?" Barbra asked. "These are my children. This is William his little brother Jonah and his little sister Tessa."

Mom held us all close to her. "Do you all have any children?" She asked. "Oh yes we all have three as well they are all in school right now, the bus picked them up a few seconds before you came out." Barbra tells her pointing at the bus stop sign, on the gate across the street. "When will these three be enrolled in school?" She went on to ask. "I was planning to take them to school this morning until this happened." Mom tells them looking at her front door. "Well, I'm sure it was just a small trimmer maybe from the desert, welcome to California!" Joy said walking back to her house. "I will catch you all later." She said waving "It was very nice to meet you," she said with a smile. "She's a bit on the wild side, still a little young." Barbra said to them shaking her head again. "Now it was very nice to meet you all please if you need anything I don't work too much I'm off Monday's and Wednesday's I am available any time on the weekends if you need help with anything please call me," she tells mom handing her a paper with her phone number on it. She walked away with her hands in her pocket, smiling back at us all. "Come on mom whatever it was I'm sure we don't have to be afraid of it." William said holding his moms hand walking toward the house. She was still a little rattled walking back. "I will make you all breakfast and we will go to the school to get you guys signed up, then we will go visit dad." Mom said to the children. She walked all over the house closing all the windows doors and cabinets.

Still looking a little baffled she didn't want us to move around too much as she wasn't familiar with the house nor the neighborhood, so she was being very attentive. "You guys sit at the table." She said to the children. "Do you mind setting the table William?" "Sure, mom I can do that." He said taking the plates and placing them all in front of the chairs. "Mom after I eat can I go back upstairs to look for something I lost?" "Sure, son do you need any help looking for it? What did you lose?" She asked him, looking up in the cabinet. "Oh, just something I got as a present from Sabien before we left." He tells her sitting down. "Oh, what is it? What does it look like?" She asked. "Oh yeah it was just a toy." He tells her. "Hmm okay." She said walking over to the table with the pan full of eggs and potatoes. "Bam!" She said, putting the food on each of their plates. After she was done, she grabbed a piece of toast from the toaster and headed upstairs. "Okay when you're done place your plates in the middle of the table and I will retrieve them when I come back, I'm just going to put on my clothes I'll be right back." She tells them walking the upstairs. William walked up as soon as he was done with his eggs and potatoes. He ate the toast as fast as he could gulping down a little orange juice and wiping his mouth quickly. "Okay guys I will be right back," he tells his siblings. They both ate as if they didn't hear him, just when he got to the tip of the stairwell, he heard the hand drum. He stopped, looking upward as if it was coming from the top of the stairs only it sounds as if it were from the garage door. He stepped back walking over to the garage door. Just as he begins to touch the knob his mother screamed out his name, "William!" She said loudly. "Do not open any doors until I get down there" She screamed out to him. He could hear her scrambling around upstairs hurrying to get back down to them. She started to come back down when she saw William standing stiff looking toward the small table where his siblings were sitting. "What is it!" She said running down grabbing him.

He pointed at the kitchen the lights, they were flickering, the cabinets were closing and opening it was as if someone was shutting them over and over again. "Grab your brother, hurry" she said grabbing Tessa from the small stoop chair. Her purse fell to the ground as she went down to get Tessa, she reached to grab it and it was as if someone kicked it into the kitchen. "Quick William here take her, and your brother go outside to the car don't move until I get there" She tells him "No mom just leave it, just leave it." He tells her shaking in fear. "Son, go to the car now," she said in a stern voice. William took his siblings outside, they cried out for their mother. "Mommy!" Little Jonah yelled out holding his hands out to her. "I will be there soon go on stay by the car." She tells them, she looks down on the floor of the kitchen for her purse as the lights flicker and the cabinets slam harder and harder it was light out, she could see her purse underneath the cabinet near the doorway of the laundry room, she reached down to grab it quickly from the ground, she screamed taking it to her chest running back to the front door. As she passes through the living room all the window's shattered blowing glass toward her as she went for the door it slams so hard that it seemed the house shook, she stopped closing her eyes. "Open this damn door right now!" She yelled as if she was talking to someone. "Right now!" She said grabbing the doorknob pulling it open it tugged against her as her hand turned red, she struggled to keep it open, back and forth she pulled and tugged until it shut locked as if it was sealed, she couldn't even open it at all anymore. She knocked on the door with her fist yelling. "Open this door right now I need to get to my babies, right now!" She said crying out, the door unlocked, it pushed her back. She grabbed her purse from the flooring running out to the car. "Get in, get in!" She yelled out. William grabbed for the door holding onto Tessa. "Mom, you have to unlock it!" He tells her, she put her hands into her purse frantically searching for the keys. She opened the doors without even taking them out, grabbed Tessa from William's hands, placing her inside her car seat. "Quickly boys get into your seats buckle up now!" She said, she reached over to Jonah buckling him in and dashed into her seat as quickly as she could, looking at the windows wide open and shattered she backs away from the house dashing down the street. "Mom what happened?" William asked her she cried as they drove alone wiping her tears away from her face listening to her navigation system telling her how to get to dads' job. "Mom will we be okay?" William asked, "Son we will be, we just have to get to dad" she tells him. She drove on until they came to the base where mom showed her Identification to get inside. "Where can I find the USS Duluth." She asked the guard. "You will need to go to pier seven." He told her. "Just go around this turn here, and instead of taking the circle all around just go to the end of the circle and keep going straight until you reach the end of the dock, you'll see the pier numbers on the flag poles of every block, just make sure you look up from time to time they're easy to miss, oh and ma'am welcome to naval base San Diego." He said to her flagging her through. Mom got to pier seven easy, she parked in the parking lot facing the ship. "We will wait here until your dad gets off work." She told them ."You think when we go back home mom things will be better? Whatever's in there will be gone when dad comes home, right?" Jonah asked. "I don't know." Mom said shaking her head looking straight ahead at the ship. "What do you think it was mom, what happened?" William asked. "I don't know son and what we don't know won't hurt us." She said leaning back in her seat with tears running from her eyes in disbelief of what happened.

Feathers In the Room

We waited in the car for hours for dad to come out. Mom fed us crackers from her purse, and water from the water bottles in the trunk, she was always prepared for anything. "I'm glad I had these from the trip over, aren't you guys glad I had them?" She asked the kids. "I am glad but mommy, I'm still a little hungry can we find something else to eat when dad gets in?" Jonah asked her. "Sure, we will son don't worry I will get us all something more to eat," she tells him rubbing the side if his face. Dad came walking down the pier in his uniform smiling. He was walking toward a carpool van when mom got out of the car flagging him over and calling his name. "We're over here honey we're over here!" She yelled out. Dad came walking looking confused kissing mom on the cheek, she grabbed onto him hugging him tight. "Honey what's wrong,? What are you doing here?" He asked her standing back staring her in the face. "Mitchell there's something going on in that house, things were moving, all the windows burst open, and I was locked inside, it wouldn't allow me to get to the kids." She was talking so fast dad had to slow her down. "Wait a minute Sara, what are you saying" He asked with his hand to his head "Just what do you mean" "I mean there's something going on in the house something crazy and scary" she told him. "Okay Sara let's get into the car I'm exhausted I can't even comprehend what you're telling me at the moment." They both got into the car shutting the doors. Mitchell secured his seatbelt. "Hey kids how are you guys doing today?" He asked them. "Daddy there's a monster living in our house." Little Jonah told him tapping his shoulder.

Mitchell put his hand to his head. "Sara what happened?" He asked as they drove off. She begins to cry and start to tell him all the mysterious things that went on that morning. By the time they got back to the house Mitchell was so startled by what Sara had told him he leaned frontward took a deep breath, as they drove into the driveway, Sara's mouth dropped opened, all the windows were sealed shut as if nothing ever happened there. She sat still. "Mitchell, I don't know what to tell you, all of the windows were blown out." She said pulling her door handle. "Okay I'm going in now honey come on." Mitchell tells her getting out of the car. "Okay but kids, you guys stay here while we check if it's safe." Sara tells them leaning in the car. "Mom hurry I have to use the restroom." William told her. "Okay son just don't move okay until I say so." Sara went to the front door following Mitchell, as they approached the door, they noticed a note had been left for them, it read, "The movers were here, they will be back at 5pm." Sara read out loud. "I guess we missed them." Mitchell said opening the door with his key. They went inside leaving the door wide open. They walked in, Sara right behind Mitchell holding onto his uniform shirt. "Sara nothing's out of place here and the windows are all fine." Mitchell tells her. "Are you sure something happened here?" He said, walking back out to grab the children. He took Tessa from her seat. "Come baby, mama's probably very tired from the move that's all sweetie." he said carrying her into the house grabbing Jonah by the hand. "Come on William, come use the restroom everything's fine in here Mitchell said putting Tessa onto the carpet.

"Come on Sara, lets relax and wait until the movers come." Mitchell went upstairs to his room to change before the movers came. Sara stood there looking around at the windows with her hand on her hip, she shook her head. "Babe don't stress yourself out maybe you're just really tired." Mitchell said to her, coming back downstairs. "We have had quite a few very busy days, and we just got here." The kids all sat around on the floor in the living room area with Sara, they were still a bit scared over what happened that morning. They really didn't know what was to come next. They sat very close to Sara waiting for the movers to come. Dad walked around the outside of the house, the backyard was big, the neighbors had swing sets and a trampoline for their children to play. Mitchell stood on the porch looking over when the man next door came out with a cigarette in his hand and a can of beer. "Hey!" He said waving up his beer at Mitchell. "Hey how are you?" Mitchell said, "I'm good man my names Brandon, welcome to the neighborhood, if you ever need anything let me know" he said, walking over to a patio set that sat in front of the slide in door.

"Sure, man nice to meet you." Mitchell said walking back into the house, he could hear the trucks pulling up as he closes the door. "I guess they're here honey." He said to Sara walking toward the front door. "They are," she said leaping up from the floor, picking up Tessa walking her over to the door. William and Jonah were still sitting when William heard the hand drum beating, this time it was coming from upstairs. He jumped to his feet running up the stairs. When he got to the top of the stairs, he could hear it getting louder. He ran into his room looking all around, as he got closer to his bag, he could hear the beating of the drum's strings and beads, he shook his bags out, one after the other. "Ugh! Where are you?" He yelled underneath his breath. Just then he walked over to his closet door attempting to open it. When he reached out his hand for the doorknob it opened wide, out came two big feathers, one black and brown the other red and orange. He watched as the feathers fell to the ground. He was still looking at them drop. He tried to close the closet door up, but it wouldn't close. He reached down for the two feathers, as he reached down, he looked into the darkened closet and in the darkness stood a tall figure dressed in Native American style clothing, it was a Native American man, brown face, with a feathered wrap around his head. He put his finger to William's mouth. "Shh!" He said, bending over snatching the two feathers from his hand and closing the closet door shut. William stood still in shock at what he'd seen, he couldn't move.

He could hear his mother and father directing the movers to bring his furniture into his room. "That goes into that room, and that stuff over there." Sara tells them holding the baby on her side. "William they're coming in make sure you've picked up all your clothes please!" Sara called out to him. William stood still standing in front of the closet door, he closed his eyes he had to open it to see if the Indian man was still there. He quickly turned the doorknob, opening the door as fast as he could. It was dark inside the closet. William looked inside, quickly peeking in all the way, looking for the Indian man. He could hear his mother coming with the movers. He began to scramble around the room picking up his clothes, tossing them all into the closet bundles at time. "Okay mom, bring it all in! He yelled out staring into the closet door. "Here and there and don't worry about putting it together, my husband will do most of that work." She told them walking out of the room for them to get the rest of the furniture. After they set William's bed up and his chest dresser he ran out of the room, he wanted to tell his mom what he saw, but he was afraid to. He knew his dad wouldn't believe any of it, he just thought they were all seeing things and hearing things. It was a new environment, it couldn't be anything other than them adjusting, dad was funny that way. He didn't believe in the supernatural things people talked about, he'd always laugh and joke and say that they were probably drinking too much, or they were tired that day, seeing things, that's all.

William watched as the movers set everything up the way mom wanted it. He was so shaken by what he'd seen in his closet he could hardly think straight. The movers were still moving things in when the school bus came. William watched from the window. The kids who lived in the neighborhood getting off the bus. There was a lot of kids in the neighborhood his age. He stood watching as the kids pointed at the big truck in front of their house they were saying, "New neighbors!" They all wondered if there were other children there, as they passed by, they each took a long look at the house before walking to their houses. When the movers began to bring the toys out, Jonah ran when he saw his bike he went and jumped on with his training wheels scraped the street dragging along with him. he begins to ride in the cul-de-sac. He was so happy to have his toys now, Tessa jumped around in moms' arms laughing at Jonah as he rode around the street. William was still looking up at his window wondering about the Native American man in his closet. When evening came, mom and dad were putting things away in the garage, Tessa fell asleep on the couch while mom worked around the house. Jonah was now running around and around the house playing with the toys he found in the boxes. William helped a little here and there, but mostly sat wondering looking up at the stairwell. He knew he'd have to go to bed soon, the

Native American man may come back. What is it that he wanted? he wondered. He continued to help his mom and dad put things away. Soon they sat for dinner, taking a small break.

"Isn't it nice to have our things home with us?" Mitchell said, passing around the bread for mom to make him a sandwich. "It is nice" Sara said to him putting mayo on his sandwich. As they all sat and ate Jonah kept moving his toy away from him with his foot, but it would come back to him as if he was kicking it to someone and they were kicking it back. He was getting up and down from the table laughing. "Sit Jonah stop that and eat!" Dad said to him. Mom saw what was going on from the corner of her eye. She watched as the toy would come back to Jonah, she watched as he kicked it away from him, this last time she quickly jumped from her seat going to grab the toy. "No more Jonah, enough eat your food." She said picking the toy up from the floor placing it on the counter. When she sat back down Jonah put his head down pouting. "Eat your food son stop pouting." Dad tells him. Jonah grabs his sandwich and puts it into his mouth, chewing slowly when he just began to laugh. Food flew from his mouth like crazy as he fell all over his chair laughing as if someone was tickling him all over. "Jonah stop that!" Dad yelled. "Stop that son and eat your food!" Jonah tries to sit up straight then begins giggling all over again. "I was thinking Sara why can't we keep the television in the den area instead of the living room?" Dad asked mom. "No, I don't want a television in there." She tells him finishing her dinner, Mom stood up from the table. Jonah got down from the table behind her, walking over to the kitchen to grab the toy. "Oh no son." Mom said to Jonah. "You have to take a bath then you can have the toy back." She tells him grabbing it before he could get it. Jonah looked up at the wall near the sink and shook his head. Mom looked over there to see what he was shaking his head at. "Why are you shaking your head Jonah?" Mom asked him. Jonah skipped off heading upstairs for his bath.

Mom grabbed Tessa from her seat and walked upstairs behind him. "William you should take a bath too when we're done you can take one up here, you need one tonight, we will go to the school in the morning no matter what happens." She tells him. When she gets to the top of the stairs she hears Jonah in the bathroom, the waters running, she could hear him jumping up and down. "Jonah what are you up to?" She says entering the bathroom. "I just want to take my bath mommy." Jonah tells her holding his hand behind his back. "What you got there?" Mom asked him sitting Tessa down on the floor of the bathroom reaching out for Jonah's arms. "Hey, let me see son," she said pulling at his arm, he resists as she pulls his arms forward. "Jonah come on what is it?" she said in her stern voice. Jonah's looking away at the water flowing from the bathtub. "No mommy we want to play with it in the bathtub" he tells her pulling his arms away from her, throwing the toy from downstairs into the water. He turns and looks at her. "Now don't you go in the water and get it mommy; you will be sorry." Jonah tells her standing looking at the toy floating in the tub. "Jonah, move away from the tub now!" Sara tells him in her stern voice. She pushes him out of the way of the bathtub, she gets on her knees reaching into the tub for the toys. As she reaches, they seem to move away from her quickly down into the water. She reaches down to grab them splashing water all over her shirt. She tries to catch the toys, it seemed as if someone was splashing water into her face, all over her really. She places both her hands into the water catching one of the toys. She felt someone clutching her wrist and twisting them tight, squeezing so tight that her hands begin to go numb. Sara screamed out "Mitchell help me!" She screams. Jonah stood by watching as if he was in shock. When Mitchell entered the bathroom, Sara was sitting on the floor, whatever was holding her wrist had let go. She held her hands to her face looking down onto the floor of the bathroom. Her wrist was bruised and bloody. "Now do you believe me Mitchell?" She screamed holding her wrist out to him, she got up from the floor of the bathroom, grabbing Tessa running out into the hallway. She ran to her room and slammed the door. William watched from the hall. Mitchell went into the bathroom and turned off the water looking down at Jonah. "Son what happened to mommy?" He asked Jonah. "I told her to leave the toys, we want to play with them in the bathtub." He tells him. "We? who's we?" He asked Jonah. "Me and Shadow daddy, my new friend shadow is here," he said to Mitchell, looking up at the wall as if someone was standing next to him.

More Than One

"Son who is Shadow?" Mitchell asked Jonah. "I told you daddy my new friend, he said you told him to come here." "No son I don't know anyone by the name Shadow." Mitchell got the bath water just right for Jonah and put him in. He took the toys out. "Son I'm curious, is this new friend from around here?" He asked him. "No daddy." He said looking upward as if he was listening to someone instruct him to answer. Mitchell quickly snapped his fingers in front of Jonah's eyes. "Son look over here I'm here," he said standing over him waving his hand in his face and snapping his finger. Jonah looked at him and smiled. "Daddy don't be afraid Shadow's a nice guy." He tells Mitchell. "Okay son, I guess maybe he is, especially when you smile like that." Mitchell got down on his knees and began to play with the toy car that he'd took alongside the bathtub. "Son I'm going to wash you up now, okay?" Mitchell washed Jonah up with soap washing his hair and rinsing him with the shower head. Mitchell stood up after reaching for the towel to dry Jonah off. "Daddy can Shadow sleep in my room with me tonight?" He asked looking up as if he was taking instructions again. "Oh, son I don't know." Mitchell said grabbing him from the bathtub. "Come son let's get you into your PJ's." Mitchell carried Jonah into his room.

Jonah walked around with his toy truck in his hand while his dad looked in the drawers for his pajama's. Mitchell watched Jonah from the corner of his eye as he seemed to be talking to himself while moving the toy back and forth from the bed to the floor. "Okay son I got them" Mitchell said to him grabbing him from his feet, placing him onto the bed. "I love you, you love me, we're a happy family." Mitchell recited a song from a previous TV show Jonah would watch every day. Jonah looked at Mitchell as if he didn't know the song. "Come on son sing it with me." Mitchell recited the song again while putting Jonah's clothes on him. Jonah looked at him and shaking his head no pointing up at the wall. "Daddy Shadow doesn't like that song please stop singing it," he said to his dad. Mitchell grabbed onto Jonah. "Hmm a friend who doesn't like this song, I don't know Jonah your friend doesn't sound friendly at all." Mitchell told him, placing him in the bed. "Okay son you really have to sleep, now tell your friend goodnight." He tells him taking the toys away and kissing him on the forehead. "Goodnight son." Mitchell said standing near the light, Jonah closed his little eyes turning on his side pulling his small blanket into his chest.

"Goodnight daddy." Jonah said yawning. Mitchell pulled the door closed leaving just a crack in it to listen throughout the night. Mitchell walked down the hallway away from Jonah's room when his little fire truck came rolling by him, the engine blared, the siren and lights flashed on and off as it went flying by his feet. Mitchell stuck his foot out to stop it from going toward the baby's room so that it wouldn't wake them. Still wondering where it came from, he walked back over to Jonah's room to check if he was still in bed. Picking the toy fire engine up from the floor, he walked slowly toward the room door to check, as he moved closer to the door it slammed shut right in his face. He reached for the doorknob thinking Jonah was up playing around, he was both angry and curious. He twisted the doorknob opened but it wouldn't budge, he yelled out for Jonah. "Jonah open up!" He yelled out. "It's daddy son open up!" Just when he began to panic, the door opened, he walked inside quickly going over to Jonah's bedside. "Son!" He said leaning over to check to see if Jonah was up. He was sound asleep. Mitchell placed the fire engine down on the dresser, he leaned in kissing Jonah on the cheek. "Goodnight son" he said again, this time he waited, watching to see if Jonah could be playing Opossum. Walking away from the room, he was curious about the fire engine looking back at it wondering how it got into the hallway. Mitchell went into the bedroom he was still very skeptical about all that his wife has been telling him, about what's been going on in the house. However, after spending time with Jonah watching him with his new friend and the runaway fire truck he's starting to wonder if what Sara is seeing around the house was a real thing or just her imagination.

Mitchell went to sleep that night on edge. As they slept soundly in the house down the hall, standing in the walkway of the stairs, stood a shadowed figure peeking into the babies' room. William got up to got to the restroom only to see this figure staring into the room. He walked past, rushing to relieve himself, with his eyes half open, he glanced at it squinting his eyes. While he stood over the toilet bowel to open it, he began to pee, thinking it must have been dad checking in on the baby, yawning looking straight down, then straight up he heard footsteps coming toward him, he flushed the toilet put the toilet seat down, turning to walk back to his room. As he reached for the doorknob to shut it behind him, there was the figure tall as can be staring at him with a painted face, red, white, and brown feathers covered the head of the figure. William stood still as he could in shock. The man was a Native American man from head to toe, he stood, feathers on his ankles, his wrist white, dotted paint dressed his face so perfectly. He looked at William nodding his head up as if he were answering a question when William began to run and scream, he grabbed him by the mouth pulling him into the bathroom.

"Shh!" The man told him covering his eyes. William was so scared his heart raced, his knees buckled underneath him he felt himself falling to the floor of the bathroom, he still tried calling out for his mother and father his eyes spread wide open in fear. He began to kick and scream and trying to bite the hands and fingers of the Indian man he could feel his heart his breathing became heavier and heavier as he fought soon the man let go dropping him to the floor of the bathroom standing over him. He began to speak to him in a language that William hadn't ever heard before. The Native American man grabbed his beaded necklace from his neck and broke it over William, dust flew at him into his eyes. William began to cry and rub his eyes in a panic, the man smiled as his eyes became blurry, too blurry to see. William stood to his feet swaying back and forth as if he was intoxicated trying to find the doorknob to get away from the bathroom. "Dad!" He yelled rubbing his eyes. "Dad help me please!" He yelled out louder and louder his mom and dad came running from their bedroom. "William! Son what's wrong! What's wrong!" They yelled running toward him. William rubbed his eyes in a panic his parents grabbed at his hand. "Son what's going on talk to us!" His dad said to him pulling on his arms. "What happened to your eyes son look at me!" He yelled pulling his hands away from his face. William blinked his eyes over and over, everything was blurred around him, he blinked faster. "William talk to me son, what happened, what's going on with your eyes?" His dad yelled to him. William's vision began to come clearer, his eyes closed shut tight then back opened wide. "William what's wrong son?" His mother yelled out, grabbing his arms squeezing them tight. William opened his eyes wide, what he saw standing down the hall was not just one Native American man dressed in all the feathers, but at least 10 of them standing together in a straight line. At the end of the line in the very back was the tallest man, standing, smiling and nodding his head shaking the hand drum over their heads. William pointed at them in shock his parents stood still unable to see what William was pointing at. It seemed he was in a trance of some sort. Mitchell stood in front of William grabbing his finger, slapping his face with his other hand. "William enough, wake up!" He said squeezing his cheeks as hard as he could, but William didn't budge instead he fell to his knees covering his eyes.

See Nothing

The next few days were so quiet, Jonah would play around with shadow all over the house, while mom and dad worked together to put things together around the house, hanging pictures and putting away houseware, staging the furniture just right. No television was allowed in the living room, but in the den area they hung the television over the fireplace. Tessa enjoyed watching all her TV programs throughout the day. You could catch her singing along with the characters every now and then. William wouldn't look up, feeling as if he may see them again, he was so scared thinking that something was wrong. He was still unable to find the hand drum, and he searched just about everywhere he could, even in the old boxes. Mitchell went to work late every day after checking all around the house for Sara who swore she couldn't be left alone for too long before things begin to happen. She would walk around the house with Mitchell early in the morning making sure he didn't miss anything. Things had gotten a little better, the kids would start school that Monday it would only be her and baby Tessa at home for hours during the day. All the neighborhood kids went to the same school unless they were in the high school or chose to go in a different district. Sara became very close with the neighbors, Barbra and her husband Eric. They were smokers, most mornings after the school bus would pull off with the children they'd sit together on their porch and smoke cigarettes until Eric had to leave to work.

Barbra would invite Sara over for a cup of coffee, she reluctantly went, in fear of all the smoking would be bad for the baby. She'd go just so she didn't have to go back into the house alone. They were very pleasant, they never smoked inside and was very careful not to smoke in front of young Tessa, and Barbra made a decent cup of coffee. They were from Kentucky, had two children, and a lot of dogs and cats. Their dogs would run up and down the stairs around the house as if they were chasing someone. Barbra said they began doing that when we moved in, and that they had been doing it all day sometimes. She didn't know why; they'd even get scared and hide up under the kitchen table. She told Sara it was normal; They'd only been there in housing for a little over four years. Her husband had done three tours in Iraq as well as having two years on sea tours. Barbra talked about how she missed Kentucky, but she was in love with California. Sara stayed over for as long as she could on weekdays when she'd go back home it would be a few hours before she had to pick up the children. She would make baby Tessa a small lunch, turn the television on and eat with her while watching the clock. Sometimes she'd just sit on the porch with Tessa letting her play ball or play with her toys on the front lawn. It was very troubling she never knew when these strange things would happen, she only knew that she didn't want to have the kind of encounter she had when they first moved in.

It was around 1:30pm, she began to clean baby Tessa up after lunch. She wiped her face and hands; she went over to the sink to put away the cloth and wash her hands when she heard the doorbell ring. She dropped the paper towel, grabbing baby Tessa from her little highchair running to the door, she wasn't expecting anyone. She looked out of the peephole, there was a UPS man standing there. "Can I help you?" She called out to him. "Ah yes I have a package for you to sign for." "Okay hold on sec." She said taking Tessa to the couch to put her down. She walked over to the door, opened it, greeting the UPS man with a smile. "Sorry about that." She said taking the pen from his hand to sign for the package. "No worries, Miss we do this all the time." The UPS man said handing her the package. "Have a good day she said closing the door, walking over to the table to place the package down, looking to see what it was before she sat it down. "Hmm they sent us a gift I bet!" She said walking over to get Tessa from the couch, Tessa was gone. "Baby where are you?" She began to run around the room into the kitchen first, then up the stairs, running as fast as she could. "Tess! Where are you sweetie! Answer me!" She yelled out. Tessa wasn't talking very much outside of mommy, daddy, mine and eat her vocabulary wasn't that great yet. She franticly began to search every room in the house in a panic. She was tearing through all the rooms everywhere upstairs. She began to cry knowing that this could be another moment where things happen, and she doesn't know what to do.

She stood by the table looking under it, then into the hallway closet, and in all the bottom kitchen cabinets, even in the oven. She looked everywhere. She sat down with her hands to her head, she began to cry and scream out, "Tessa where are you baby girl tell mommy!" She yelled out crying, suddenly she heard Tessa laughing. It sounded as if it was coming from the garage. She hadn't search there. She jumped from her seat, running toward the garage door when she heard the laughing again, this time it sounded as if it was coming from the backyard. "Tessa!" She went into the garage anyway hoping to find her underneath the car or anywhere she could. She looked everywhere, still the laughing from baby Tessa began to get louder. She looked up, she could hear the laughter and heavy walking. It sounded as if there were people walking around upstairs. She ran upstairs to see if there was someone there, searching again all over the rooms, from one room to the next she ran all around crying, looking for who could have been walking around. Still following the sound of Tessa's laughter, she went into Tessa's room, and stood around waiting to hear the footsteps again. There was none. She cried out for Tessa again. What would she do if she couldn't find her? She sat on the bed looking out of the window. She could see the neighbors all coming outside to wait for the school bus. She looked down at her watch glancing over at the door. She saw a figure standing in the doorway staring back at her. It was a woman dressed in a white and blue dress with boots on, she looked as if she was from another time. Her hair was pinned up in a neat roll, she winked at Sara and walked away. Sara stood to her feet startled at what she'd seen. She walked slowly toward the door to follow the woman when she reached the hallway, the woman stood down the hall with her back turned to the other end of the hallway. She turned to Sara slowly, in her arms she held Tessa up to her face.

She rubbed her nose to Tessa's, placed her on the floor, and in a very demonic voice she screamed out to Sara, "Don't leave your baby!" Sara ran toward Tessa, reaching for her, scooping her up from the ground. The woman walked away into the wall looking back at them. Sara ran for the stairwell down to the front door to greet the school bus. She grabbed her bag as well, she refused to go back inside until Mitchell got home at 4pm. She greeted the children telling them to go to the car, they were going for a ride to get food until daddy gets home. "Mom, I met some of the neighborhood kids today," William tells her. "I wanted to do my homework and see if I could hang out with them at the playground in the back?" He asked Sara looked at him in the rearview mirror. "William not today

honey, now buckle up please and help your brother please."
She said looking at the house. She looked up at the
bedroom window where Tessa's room was, she hadn't
strapped Tessa in, still contemplating whether she wanted
to go to the store to buy more groceries or the mall where
she could shop, and the kids could eat and play while they
wait for Mitchell to get home. When she made up her mind
she took Tessa into her arms, placed her in her car seat
strapping her in tight, looking up at the window thinking
about that pioneer woman staring at her, yelling at her in
that voice. She closed the door got in and drove off. Sara
cried all the way to the store. She felt like she was losing
her mind. All these things happening all while they just got
into this new house. She passed many churches along the
way to the mall thinking should she go in to speak to a
priest? Should she ask what they thought of all the things
going on around the house? After all Mitchell didn't
believe any of it.

When she got back home that evening Mitchell was
there cleaning the front porch. He began watering the grass.
"Sara where have you been? I've been calling you and
calling you, I thought something was wrong. I was so
worried when I saw that you had left your cell at home,
where were you?" He asked her as he walked up to the car.
"I had some things to do, some errands to run." She told
him getting the kids from the car, unstrapping their
seatbelts telling them to go in and get washed up for dinner.
"But you left your cell Sara." Mitchell said to her,
following her into the house carrying Jonah on his hip.
"Hey son!" He said kissing Jonah on the forehead. "Hi
dad!" Jonah said as he placed him down on the floor. "Hi
dad!" William said. "Hi son how was school today?" He
asked him. "It was good dad; I met some new friends today

they live across the street." He told him going into the kitchen. "Mom wouldn't let me play with them today though, we had to go to the mall." Sara went to the kitchen right away carrying Tessa in her arms. "Do you think you can grab the groceries from the car for me please?" She asked Mitchell. "Of course, honey but first a kiss." He said pouting his lips, grabbing her by the face with his hands. "I missed you honey, I will get the stuff, but when I come back you must tell me what's eating you. I can tell somethings wrong. I hope it's something about a bun in the oven." He said walking toward the front door. "There will be no buns in this oven I promise you, this is all you get, enjoy!" She said holding Tessa close to her chest. She was almost afraid to put Tessa down in the house after what happened today, and she really didn't want to share her experience with Mitchell knowing how he felt about the supernatural.

She placed Tessa down in her highchair sitting next to her, hoping she doesn't move. Even if she had to get up to cook, she just wasn't feeling good about what happened today. She waited at the table with Tessa until Mitchell came in with the bags. "Hey, can you feed her fruit while I get dinner on, please?" She asked him. "Sure, but only if you share with me what's going on in that pretty little head of yours." He said kissing her again, holding her this time whispering into her ear. "When will we be expecting?" He asked her. "Mitchell!" she said pushing him away. "There's no news of a baby coming anytime soon I promise, this is it." She said to him going over to the sink to wash out a bowel to clean the vegetables in. "This is it for us, our family is complete!" She tells him washing the bowel. "I think I want more, baby." Mitchell tells her sitting at the table with Tessa, he tapped her little nose. "Don't you want a sister?" He said. Tessa looked over his head as if she was looking behind him. "Sister!" She said pointing her little finger. "Sister, sister, sister!" She said repeatedly. "No sweetie, in mommy's tummy see in there." He tells her pointing at Sara's tummy. "No daddy sister!" She said pointing behind him. Mitchell turned around looking across the room at what her little fingers were pointing at. He saw a shadow of a figure in the living room, he stood to his feet quickly, going to see what it was. He looked around curiously wondering if the boys were playing a trick on him. Sara took notice. "Honey what's wrong, you see something?" She asked him, holding a pair of bell peppers in her hand. "No there's nothing there." "Are you sure you don't see anything?" She asked. "No there's nothing." He said pushing his chair toward Tessa's. "Hmm, I saw something early today, maybe it wasn't really there either." Sara said turning back to the sink washing the lettuce and bell peppers. "Only it spoke." She said under her breath. "What did you say honey?" "Nothing honey, I saw nothing either."

Fire and Feathers

Sara was so scared, she carried Tessa on her hip everywhere she went in the house from that day on, afraid to leave her alone anywhere. She even took her into the bathroom with her when she showered and used the restroom. She would sit Tessa in her activity chair right in front of the bathroom door, especially when Mitchell was working. Sara spent even more time at the neighbors every day. She knew that even if they smoked it was outside, the baby wasn't in any danger, but she could tell some days that the Bennet's didn't always want her company. She tried not to be around to much when Eric was home, but Eric worked at night he was an IT guy for the Navy. He was home a lot throughout the day and would only go into work like a civilian at times. His job wasn't as hectic as Mitchell's was although quite important. Eric had ranked very high on the pay grade as well and was a bit of a nerd. He was always talking to Barbra about many ways that the computers were changing. He'd sit sometimes in the living room of their home at a desk, near the window with several computers placed in front of him. Each computer was from a different brand. He had them all, old ones, new ones, fast ones, slow ones. He would sit there for hours before work just working on them, talking to Barbra about what they all could do different. At times Barbra would rush to the door when Sara showed up, rolling her eyes opening the door. "You saved me please come in!" She'd say, holding the screen door open for her and Tessa. "I have coffee, let's go in the kitchen." She'd say. She would be overwhelmed with the conversation her and Eric were having. Sara would laugh telling her, "You're so lucky though, he's here with you almost all the time, I miss Mitchell every second of the day." She'd tell Barbra.

"Oh honey, you're still in love huh" Barbra would respond smiling "Sit down sweetie tell me what's going on, do you plan on working, what is it that you do professionally?" Barbra asked.

"Oh, when we met, I was a second-grade teacher." "Was?" Barbra questioned. "Oh yeah because of the Navy and after having William, Mitch and I agreed that it would just be better for us if I was to stay home and raise the kids, you know because the job takes him away a lot." She said sipping her coffee "Hmm honey that's good but are you happy doing this? I mean your baby is attached at the hip, do you ever put her down on the floor?" Barbra looked at Sara crossed. "Oh yeah she's just a little sleepy right now, getting the kids out early sometimes it wears her out in the morning." She tells Barbra. "Oh, I see, so is there something you like to do? California has so much to offer during the day, here look in there the base offers all kind of classes, mommy and me exercise classes and more." She said sipping her coffee, holding her cigarette in between her fingers. "Hanging around here all day will drive you insane." She tells her looking over at Eric. Sara began to feel uncomfortable, feeling as if Barbra was dismissing her politely. "Well, I can see you are super busy today." Sara said taking one last sip of her coffee, placing it on the table, clutching baby Tessa to her hip then grabbed the paper from the table walking to the door. "So, will I see you tomorrow?" Barbra said to her walking behind her. "No, I think I will go and check out these classes." Sara told her. Barbra closed the door behind them, watching her walk away through the window. She turned to Eric. "Is it time?"

She asked him. "It is!" Eric told her, turning off all the computers in front of him, then he closed all the windows. Barbra snatched off her shirt and begin to run upstairs with Eric chasing behind her. They would make love until it was time for Eric to leave for work. The dogs and the cats would follow them upstairs, waiting at the stairs and watching the door. The dogs were shaking at every scream Barbra made, she was a screamer when they made love. Eric was boring and nerdy at times, but it never mattered when they made love. Barbra was completely satisfied with him. When they finished the dogs would be jumping at the door. Barbra would come out, they'd follow her down to the kitchen to get treats and she would put them outside except for the cats, the cats were spoiled, sitting at the dinner table waiting for their treats. They often sat in the window waiting for Barbra to come in from outside with the dogs. Barbra went back upstairs after giving them their treats she'd get onto the shower with Eric before work they'd make love again. When they were done Eric would put on his uniform and rush out to his car to get to work. Barbra would take her time getting dressed laying across the bed sometimes without her clothes on, just her robe. She would enjoy a little peace before the children would come home from school. On this day she laid across the bed watching from the window as Eric drove away. She could hear the dogs scratching the door to come back inside from having their snack.

She got up, wrapped her robe around her waist walking down the stairs to the kitchen, there she found her five cats all laying on the table dead. They were laid out in a circle and in the middle, there was feathers. Barbra screamed very loud covering her eyes. She ran for the door; she couldn't believe what she was seeing. She ran as fast as she could for the front door, running out toward Sara's house. "Help me! Help me! my cats are dead!" She said crying. "All of them they're all dead!" She told Sara. Sara opened the door quickly. "What's wrong what do you mean?" She asked her. "They're dead Sara, my cats are all dead! I was upstairs getting dressed, when I came down, they were there on the table dead!" Okay let's call base security." She tells Barbara. "I have the number on the fridge." She grabbed baby Tessa up from the floor. "Hold on come in Barbra sit." She told her. "Don't worry we will find out what's going on." She told her. The dogs were barking so loud by now looking for Barbra, they were in a panic. "I should go, my dogs are looking for me, do you hear them?" She said wiping her eyes. "What if something happens to them too?" She said standing to her feet. "Hold on Barbra, hold on, I will call them, we can go get the dogs together." Sara told her dialing security from her cell phone.

"Yes, we need security right away, 1081 Truett Lane." She told them. "I will explain when they get here, please hurry!" She said hanging up the phone. "Okay Barbra let's go get the dogs, we can bring them here while we wait for security to come." Sara said. Barbra stood outside the door waiting for Sara crying her eyes out. The other neighbors saw them come out of the house and noticed Barbra crying and ran over to them. "Barb are you okay?" Joy asked. She shook her head no. "Something happened to the cats." Sara told them, passing by them going to the house. "What happened?" Joy asked. "Not now Joy, sorry, we are just going to grab the dogs and take them over to my house to wait for security." Sara told her, clutching little Tessa onto her hip holding onto Barbra's hand. "Okay I will call you Barbra, I'm sorry." Joy said walking back over to her house. When they arrived at Barbra's door it was wide open. "I can't go in there." She said shaking her head crying. "Okay then, I will go in, can you hold Tessa for me? I will go grab them and we will get out of here." Sara told her, removing Tessa from her hip. Baby Tessa was squirming around, she wasn't used to Barbra. She pushed away as Sara handed her over. "It's okay baby, mommy will be right back, I promise, you stay right here with Miss Barbra, mommy will be back." She told her going into the house. She walked in through the living room and into the kitchen. She was very quiet passing through; she didn't want to look at the cats on the table. She just glanced at them laying there, still with no blood, they looked like stuffed animals wrapped around the table in a perfect circle with feathers in the middle of them as if someone was forming a pattern of some sort. Sara walked over to the glass slide-in door where the dogs were barking. She opened the door, they rushed in racing for the front door to greet Barbra. Sara raced behind them to make sure she didn't put Tessa on the ground in her excitement to see her dogs. Sara grabbed Tessa from Barbra's hands. "There you go, see they're safe, let's go to my house and wait for security, wonder what's taking them?" Sara said as they walked back over to her house. When they got to the door the dogs stood still at the front door, refusing to go into the house with Barbra. They began to cry and shake at the doorway.

"Come on go inside!" Barbra told them taking the smaller dog on the floor of the front entrance inside the door. The dog ran out shaking and crying. "What the devil is wrong with you?" Barbra asked him, grabbing him looking into his eyes. He was shaking in her hands; the others were now kneeling to the porch floor shaking. Barbra turned to Sara as she stood inside her house at the door waiting. "We will just wait on the porch, they are really afraid to come in, I've never seen them like this before." She said grabbing the little one to her chest, kissing his forehead sitting on the patio chair on the porch. When the security guy showed up Barbra walked him over to the house with the little dogs following behind her. They all seemed to be afraid to leave her side. They went inside. Barbra stood by the door while Sara went over to watch. The security officer was alone, he went inside and came back out quickly. "Ma'am I am going to take some photos is that okay?" He asked Barbra. "Of course, but can you tell what happened, did someone come inside my home?" ''Ma'am I'm going to call the local police department it seems as if they may have." The officer told her getting on his radio requesting the military police and the local police. He was fascinated by what he saw. He couldn't believe his eyes at all, he kept pacing up and down the sidewalk in front of the house while waiting for the police to show up. When they arrived, they all stood in front of the house talking for a few seconds before going in. They went in one by one, the humane society van showed up as well.

Two women from the humane society walked up with bags in their hands. "Hi, do you live here? I'm Cat, sorry for your loss." She said holding out her hand to shake Barbra's hand. The little dog shook and barked at the women as they began to ask their questions. "Ma'am how many animals do you have in total?" She asked. "I have in all, eight animals, five cats and three dogs." She said sniffling with tears dropping from her eyes. "I'm so sorry I promise this won't take long." The other woman said. "My name is Taylor Ma'am; we will go in and remove the cat's. We will place them in individual bags and later after we get them to the humane society you can come there to figure out what you want to do with them, we just need you to sign a few forms, we will take some photos as well." Taylor said to her in a calm voice. "Okay I just want to know how they died, what happened to them, I just left them at the table eating their breakfast, just let me know how they died." "Of course, we will. They said tapping her on the shoulder going into the house. They walked in engaging the police officers. "Wow, what do we have here?" Cat asked, "It's really strange right, it's as if they were placed there like that." The security officer said to them. "Yeah, is this lady okay?" They whispered, "I've really never seen anything like it and what's with the feathers?" Taylor asked, "Let's get this done and go take as many pictures as you can." The officer said looking around the house there was cat toys all around the house. They began bagging the cat's up one by one. When they were done Barbra and the dogs entered the house. Sara entered after them. Barbra continued holding onto the little dog. "I just don't know what's going on, my cats are healthy cats Sara," she said still crying.

"I'm so sorry Barbra I know this is hard." Sara said to her standing to her feet to give her a hug clutching little Tessa to her waist. "I am going to clean up a bit for you then, maybe, I can call Eric for you, and we can go to my house for a while." Sara told her walking around picking up things from the room. "Is it okay for me to wash the table off or would you like for me to leave?" "I think I can handle it, thank you so much Sara, I just want to be with the dogs I will call Eric myself, thank you for everything." She said standing up hugging Sara. She walked them to the door still sniffling and tearing up. "I will see you later sweetie thank you again." Sara went home it was a little late to feed Tessa a small lunch she rushed into the kitchen, sat baby Tessa in the highchair, and begin to make her lunch. She was so distraught over what happen to those cats. After feeding Tessa she hurried out to greet the school bus she decided today to stay at the house, just sit in the den watching television waiting for Mitch to come home. After feeding the kids and cleaning, they did just that until Mitchell got there. When he showed up Sara grabbed him hugging him so tight. "What's going on, are you okay?" Mitchell said pulling back, looking Sara in the face. "Today, Barbra next door, her cats died, they were placed in a circle on the kitchen table with feathers it was so sad, and Barbra was devastated." She told Mitchell in a whisper trying not to alert the children. "Shh!" Mitchell looked over at Jonah and William. They were both tuned into what they were watching on tv they didn't seem to be listening. Mitchell and Sara sat at the table talking when William came into the kitchen for a drink. He took one sip of his fruit drink and looked at them in a daze as if he was looking through them. "The feathers are fuel there will be fire next time." He told them looking straight. He turned, looked out of the window, took his drink to his lips, drank it all down, turned back to them with a blank stare then he walked over to them and begin to throw up all over the kitchen table. Liquid spewed from his mouth like a water fountain. Sara and Mitchell jumped to their feet. "William are you okay?" They said running around for napkins and towels. He was still throwing up liquid until it stopped. He held his head down lifting it slowly, holding his stomach. He looked at them with a smirk. He stood up tall looking straight at the walls, then out from his mouth as if it was liquid came colorful long feathers, all over the kitchen they flew. Sara and Mitchel stood in silence, in shock of what they saw. Mitchell grabbed onto Williams shoulders. There was nothing he could do but hold onto his son.

Fire

They were the same feather that were placed in the middle of the cats that day. Sara grabbed William and held him tight. Mitchell stood in complete silence for a while not knowing what to say or do. He stood by the table looking down at the feathers all over the floor. Sara shook William. "Are you okay!" She yelled. "William are you okay?" She asked him again. William's eyes rolled back he began to shake. Sara screamed out, "Mitch, Mitch! Help me! William!" Mitchell picked William up from his feet and ran to the door. He put him into the car. "I'm going to the hospital. I will call you Sara stay with the kids." He said from the window of the driver seat. "I will call you." He backed out of the driveway quickly and sped off to the hospital. They were new to the city Mitchell stopped off at the gas station to put the address to the military hospital into the GPS. He was so nervous. William kept mumbling, "Help me dad help me!" He said in a whisper.

"Son I'm going to get you some help please hang on." He said as he sped out of the gas station parking lot. "Son stay with me." He said as he sped through the streets of the city. When they arrived at the hospital, he parked in the emergency parking area. He grabbed William out of the car rushing him into the hospital. "Help me please my son is sick please help!" He yelled, holding him at the counter of the reception area.

The nurses came running out, the receptionist approached Mitchell. "Sir I just need your Identification and I need you to sign for treatment." She said as the nurses began to check William out right there sitting him down into a wheelchair. They begin to triage him, checking vitals making sure he was stable, and breathing correctly. They gave him oxygen and rolled him into the back to put him into a bed. When they got back there William was up looking around as if he'd didn't know what was going on. "Dad!" He screamed. "Dad! What's going on!" He yelled out while they were trying to place an IV into his arm. "Son relax you were passed out; you've been vomiting and fainting." Mitchell tells him standing next to the bed. "We just have to get you checked out son relax." "Dad I'm okay we can go now I'm okay." William said, aware now that he would be getting a needle in his arm. "No son we have to get you checked out now just relax." Mitchell told him nodding his head at the two nurses in the room. "Sir can you tell me what brought you into the emergency room today?" The nurse asked. "Sure, he had juice after dinner after he drank the juice, he started vomiting all over the kitchen, when he stopped vomiting, he passed out." He tells her looking over at William. "Sir was there any other symptom before this happened? Did he have a fever or diarrhea?" She asked him. "No not that I know of no." "Was there anything going around in school, like a virus or stomach illnesses that you know of?" She asked him. "No but I will call my wife an ask." He told her pulling his cell phone from his pocket.

"I am not sure, but we've had a lot of the students from the high school in here with a stomach virus, sweetheart has there been any sick kids at your school?" She turned to ask William. He shook his head no. "Okay we'll run a few tests to see what's going on, my name is Annie, the doctor will be in shortly to check you out." She told Mitchell, walking around the bed inspecting what the other nurse had done. "Okay he's good for now, are you good son?" She asked William. He shook his head yes "Okay then we'll be back shortly." She told him signaling to the other nurse to go out of the door. Mitchell looked at his phone Sara had called over a dozen times, he began calling her. "Hello Mitchell, is he okay, what the doctor say?" She asked in a panic. "He is ok honey, calm down please they are saying it could have been a virus." "A virus with feathers? Mitch, you saw what I saw there are still a few feathers left around on the floor of the kitchen, didn't you tell them about the feathers?" She asked. "No Sara that would make me look insane I will not be bringing up the feathers." He said in a whisper. "Do you want us to be locked away in a crazy house? We can't tell anyone about that, no." He said in his stern voice. "Mitchell are you serious? I just explained to you that there were feathers around Barbra's dead cats, what about that, do you think that's crazy?" "Sara the doctors coming in, I will call you once we see what's wrong with him, please don't mention those feathers to me again?" He said hanging up the phone.

Mitchell sat next to William on the chair next to his bed. "Son you'll be just fine." He said rubbing his head. "Dad what happened? Why did you bring me here?" He asked him. "You became really ill after having juice, you don't remember?" "No dad I don't." He said sitting up a little in the bed looking at Mitchell. "You don't remember what you said to us about the fire and the feathers?" He asked him. "No, I don't." William said looking confused. "It's okay son just relax it doesn't matter now; we're here they will get you better." He said leaning back scratching his head again. Just then the doctor came in. "Hi how are you? My name is Doctor Roberts I'll be treating your son William today." He said looking at the chart. "So, I hear you have a bit of a stomachache?" He asked washing his hands. "Yes, a little I mean I did have one I guess that's why I'm here." "Hmm, okay, when did this start were you at school or at home?" He asked looking William over checking his eyes and ears. "Do you mind if I look under your shirt son, I just want to check your stomach." He said standing with his hands on his hips. "Dad?" William said looking for an answer. "Of course, if you must please check." Mitchell told the doctor. He pulled up William shirt and began to touch his stomach at times pushing it down on both sides. "Does it hurt here?" He asked. William shook his head no. "What about here?" He asked. William shook his head no again. "Are you having any pain when I push?" The doctor asked. "What about when I let up, does it hurt?" William shook his head no again. "Okay and the vomiting, did you feel nausea before you vomited?" He asked. "No, I don't remember." William said shaking his head. "Dad I'm okay I told you we can just go home, right?" He said to Mitchell looking at him afraid.

"I think that you have a virus, you don't have a fever and you're not in any pain at the time although this worries me that you fainted, I feel like you may have been a little dehydrated, which is what usually happens in these cases, we will wait for the test to come back and if everything comes back okay I will be alright with you going home, you're getting fluids now so that should take care of your dehydration, the nurse will come back and check on you and I will be back with all the test results we took and like I said you can go if they are all good." "Thank you doctor." Mitchell said shaking his hand. "No worries see you guys soon." He said walking out of the door looking down at the chart. "See dad he thinks I'm okay too." William said sitting up grabbing the water from the tray in front of him. Mitchell got back on his cell phone to call Sara. "Hey, he's okay they said it could be a virus and that he's dehydrated, we'll be home soon." He tells her. "And no on the feathers huh Mitch?" She says upset. "Well listen, I'm really scared we have to move out of here, there is something going on in this place and I don't feel safe." She tells him. "Okay Sara, I get it, we'll talk about it when I get home." He tells her. "Try not to worry, we'll be home in a few hours." He says hanging up the phone. They finished up with William, all the tests came back negative he was free and clear to leave. The nurse removed the IV and bandaged his arm. The doctor came in and looked him over one last time and told Mitchell to make sure and take him to see his primary doctor in a week and if the symptoms should get worse to bring him back. On the drive home Mitchell was quiet, he kept picturing what happened in his head, he just couldn't wrap his head around it.

What the hell was going on in this house? In this neighborhood? Mitchell doesn't believe in ghost, nor does he believe in spirits he was so shaken by what he saw that he almost missed the exit home, thinking about it until William yelled out, "Dad don't we need to go that way?" He said quickly. "Oh yeah son, I'm still learning these streets over here." He tells him turning onto their street slowly. "Yeah, I only know them because sometimes mommy likes to ride around after school before you get home from work, she takes drives around in circles sometimes." He tells his dad. "Really why?" He asked William as they pulled up to the house. William shrugged his shoulders. "I don't know I just think she likes to drive sometimes." He said hopping out of the car running to the house. "Mom I'm okay." He says walking into the door holding his paperwork in his hand. "Good son" His mom said standing to her feet to hug him. They were all in the den area watching television. "What are you all watching?"

Mitchell said sitting on the couch, overwhelmed at what was going on. "We were watching a kids show." She said pointing at little Jonah who was sitting on the floor in front of the television singing along to the songs. Sara sat next to Mitchell. She placed Tessa on his lap. "Honey what do we do?" She asked him, putting her head on his shoulders. They sat there with the kids noticeably quiet. Mitch would be leaving for work in a few hours, in the wee hours of the morning leaving Sara and the kids alone in the house. He thought about something happening while he was gone. He knows he wouldn't be able to live with himself if something happened to Sara and the kids.

When they went to bed that night, Sara wanted all of them to sleep in the room with her and Mitchell, but William refused, saying he was too old to sleep with his parents and he just wanted his space to be comfortable. Mitchell agreed with him, but Sara wasn't sure she would be able to rest with him down the hallway after what happened that day. She stayed up watching the door almost all through the night. Mitchell was up at 3am getting ready for work when she finally started to doze off to sleep. She could hear his footsteps all around the room, he'd kiss her on the cheek then head for the stairs. When the front door closed, she knew he was gone, she could see the lights of the car from her bedroom window, she laid there trying to sleep turning onto her back. She stared down the dark hallway at William's door dozing on and off. She was so tired and stressed she turned over onto her side, she kept hearing a popping sound as if a fire was burning, she jumped to her feet, running for Williams room. She opened the door slowly from the hallway she could see light waving orange and red, light like fire in the windows of the house. Oh no! She thought could the house be on fire? The popping noises got louder; she went into Williams room he was sound asleep. The noise was louder and there were flames glaring in the window as if there was a fire in the backyard somewhere. She ran over to the window there was nothing. When she looked out, she couldn't see all the way down into the backyard. **B**ut she could hear the popping. She ran to Jonah's room where there is a clearer view of the backyard and there, she saw one of the craziest things, in the playground behind the houses was a fire burning in the middle of the playground. The flames were so high. The flames were in a circle surrounded by dirt as if someone built a fire pit.

Sara rushed downstairs to look from the back patio door. She stood there looking out of the door. The flames burned higher and higher as she stood there. The light from the fire glared on the patio door, then suddenly out of nowhere there were five Native Americans standing all dressed in Indian style ritual feathers and clothing, staring back at her. She was startled, jumping back from the window. She began to run back up the stairs. She fell twice trying to get the children. She screamed out for William. "William wake up, come here!" She said running toward his room. Then running as quickly as she could to her room, she went to the bed pulling the covers from the kids, grabbing Tessa and Jonah. She didn't put shoes on. She grabbed her slippers and slipped them on quickly, holding Tessa in her arms and keeping Jonah close. She walked quickly to down the hall to Williams room. "William get up! Let's go now!" She yelled. "Huh, mom what?" William said lifting his head from his pillow. "Come, get up we're leaving!" She tells him, signaling him to get up, looking down the hallway making sure no one was there. "Come on son get up!" William got out of bed rubbing his eyes. "Mom where are we going? What's wrong?" He asked following her down the hall. "There's a fire, come on let's go, stop asking questions." She tells him going down the stairs. "A fire, where mom?" William said following her to the door. Just as she went to open the door there was a knock. "Police department can we talk to you?" The policeman said loudly.

Sara stood there quietly. She was startled at them being there. She held onto Tessa clutching her to her hip and pulling Jonah close. William stood close to her. "Open the door mom maybe they can help." William told her. "Shh!" Sara said squinting her eyes. "What in the world?" She said in a whisper. They knocked again, this time the knocking was more forceful. "Police anybody home!" The officer yelled out. "Yes, hold on please." Sara responded covering William's mouth. "Don't say a word when I open this door, none of you, don't say anything I will handle it." She said taking a deep breath opening the door. "Hi officer how can I help you?" She said clearing her throat. "Hi, I'm officer Bradford this is my partner Shaffer, we have been called out to your neighbor's house to investigate, they said they've been hearing some loud noises and running around in the back of the housing complex. We wanted to know if you'd been experiencing some of the same things or maybe you saw some strangers around the back? Sometimes we get some young teens around here playing games at night knocking on doors and windows scaring the families. Have you heard anything or seen anything like that?" He asked her. "Uh, no sir I have not but we just moved in, we haven't really seen too much of anyone around here." She tells them. "Okay and no knocking or banging on your windows nothing like that, right?" The other officer asked.

"No sir, sorry I can't help." "Uh ma'am were you headed out somewhere, is everything okay?" The tall officer Bradford asked." OH yes everything is fine, we were just going to take a ride to visit my parents." She tells them. William looked confused and Jonah started looking back at the kitchen table as if someone was there. "You were leaving to drive to your parent's house at this hour ma'am?" The other office asked. "Yes, you know to beat traffic, my parents live in Oregon." She tells them. "Oregon, hmm okay and no one's here in the house but you and the kid's ma'am?" He asked, "No we're here alone just leaving." He says looking around the house peeking in. "No officer we aren't alone," Little Jonah said loudly. "My friend Shadow is here," he told them looking back at the kitchen door. The officers looked at Sara. "Ma'am who is shadow, is he here with you?" "No officer no one's here but us. My son has an imaginary friend he calls shadow, no one's here." She said again reassuring them. "Oh, I see do you mind if we ask him some questions." Officer Braford didn't wait for an answer he went right on asking Jonah questions. "So, this friend Shadow where is he?" He asked. "Oh, he's out in back now but he was sleeping in my room." "Oh yeah?" The officer said smiling. "And is he tall, or short?" He asked using his hands to give him a length to go on. "He's tall and he has on a cowboy hat, cowboy boots, blue jeans and a jean jacket!" He tells them holding on to his little pajama pants moving from side to side. "Hmm ma'am, you sure you're alone? That's a pretty good description he's giving us." He said smiling. "No sir there's no one here but us and we're leaving, is there anything else you needed I really have to go now?" Sara told them pushing the children back from the doorway to close the door.

"No that's it." The officer said. "Just if you hear anything or see anything that needs to be reported please don't hesitate to give us a call." He handed her his card and began walking away. "Thank you for your time, ma'am have a safe drive." The tall officer Bradford said with a smile. "Hey kids stay safe, bye son tell that friend Shadow Hi for us." He said getting into his car. "Bye!" The kids waved as Sara closed the door. "Mom are we really going to grandma's house?" William asked. "Yes, we can go it's Friday you'll only miss one day of school." She tells them grabbing her phone and purse from the counter by the doorway. "Come on grab your brothers hand let's go." She tells them. "Mom what about dad? I just wanted to play with my friends around here, I met some friends' mom." William said reluctant to follow her out of the door. "William go to the car now grab your brother's hand." She said opening the door for them to leave. "Sheesh! Mom, I don't want to go." He said following her out of the door to the car. As she was putting Tessa into her car seat the police came back. Officer Bradford got out of the car and walked over to Sara with something in his hand. Sara buckled Tessa in safely standing up beside the car. "Ah hey! The officer said, "We wanted to give these to the kids." He said handing her a handful of stickers made like badges. "Oh, and we wanted to say thank you for your service." He said walking away, Sara waved. "Thanks!" She said walking to the driver's side of the car getting in. "Okay kids let's go, daddy will be okay until we figure things out." She said starting the car. She took a deep breath looking up at the window of the house, she pulled away from the house slowly onto the street.

Into Oregon

The drive was so long. Sara and Mitchell argued back
and forth over the phone as they drove further away from
California. Mitchell even called Sara's parents telling them
that they had to convince her to come home. He would be
leaving to do a sea tour soon and she needed to be home.
He wanted his family home before he had to go away. He
pleaded with Sara, but she wouldn't budge. They arrived in
Oregon late that evening only stopping a few times to use
the restroom and eat. Sara drove all the way into Oregon.
She felt she had to get away from whatever was haunting
them in the house. When they arrived at her parent's house,
they were waiting on the porch for her and the children.
"What a lovely surprise!" Sara's mother said greeting them
in the driveway. "I just thought I'd come home for a while
mom, good to see you." Sara said candidly grabbing her
things from the car. "Get out of the car boys, we're here."
She said to William and Jonah. "Mom we really need to go
home." William said. "I miss daddy Jonah said sliding out
from his booster in the back. "Kids come on; we'll see him
soon." Sara said walking up onto the porch where her
father was waiting. "Hey dad how's it going?" She said
approaching him for a kiss. "Oh, it's going." He responded.
"Hey sweetie, everything okay? what brings you home?"
He said grabbing Jonah up off his feet, carrying him into
the house. "Grandpa I'm too big now I can walk," he said
pulling and pushing his way back down to the floor.

They all went into the house. The house was cozy and
warm, there were pictures of Sara and her siblings and the
kids everywhere. There was all of grandpa's medals and

certificates everywhere as well. He was a highly decorated Airman in the Airforce he was very proud. Grandma got the kids settled in the kitchen for something to eat. "Are you all ready for a good meal?" She asks them placing Tessa on the countertop handing her a cookie. Tessa took a bite and smiled grabbing grandma's face kissing her. "Yes, sweetie I know they're good she said to her. "But I'm going to make you all something better." She said taking Tessa down placing her onto the floor. "Sara honey would you like some tea?" She yelled out. "Yes, mom please." She yelled back sitting on the floor next to her dad's lazy boy chair, placing her head to his knees. He put his hand on top of her head. "Sweetie whatever it is, please tell me now if it's going to send me to jail so that I can give you my bail money," he said with a smile. "No daddy." She said looking up at him with tears running from her eyes. "It's the house daddy, I don't want to be there, ever since we moved in there's been so many crazy things happening." She tells him wiping her face sitting up straight as her mom hands her a coffee cup full of tea. "I put a little honey in it sweetheart just the way you like it." She told her going back into the kitchen where the kids were, shaking her head. "I hope it's not too bad sweetie." Sara sipped her tea looking at the floor next to her dad.

"So, sweetie what's wrong with the housing? You don't have to stay you know, Mitchell can request to move you elsewhere," he tells her. "I know dad but that can take months, there's so many things happening there, it's haunted." She tells him "Haunted? You mean like a haunted house?" He asked. "Yes, daddy I think someone died there and it's not just me, the neighbors are experiencing things too." She told him placing her tea on the table near his chair. "Well, that's a story you can't tell the housing authority they'll definitely think you needed to go to the looney bin." He told her, grabbing his peanuts from the table, taking the bag to his mouth. "Hmm darling, I just don't know, maybe you're just tired maybe you need a break from the kids," he says to her. "I know when I was in the service and your mom was left alone in the house with you kids, she was almost just about batshit when I returned. Sometimes she didn't know what to do with herself." He said taking a sip of his can of juice on the table. "Daddy it's not like that, the house is really haunted, I've seen things the kids have seen things, daddy I'm afraid that the next time it comes around it will do us harm." She tells him taking her tea from the table. "Do harm? No, Sara ghost can't do harm they can only wander." He tells her. "What does Mitch say about it?" Her dad asked. "Well Mitch doesn't believe in ghost daddy he'd rather ignore them." She said putting her head to his knee again. "Well, I'm with Mitch, being in the military is already hard enough, leaving your family and trying to make ends meet it's tough, worrying about a ghost is the least of his worries sweetie. I advise you to stick it out don't allow it to scare you away from home, whatever it is will leave as soon as it knows that you're not afraid and you won't leave." He tells her rubbing her hair.

"Dad, I can't just ignore them, they are doing terrible things, the kids see them, Jonah has a friend who's a cowboy. He can describe him and everything I'm telling you daddy it's not good." She tells him. "Well, this is what I'd do sweetie, I'd go back home check the history of the house, find out what and who was there before you and go from there. You have time, you don't work. Try to find out all you can about these ghosts." He tells her smiling. "But don't allow it to scare you away." He says drinking the rest

of his V8 from the can. "Daddy no I won't live that way."
She tells him sitting up looking at him cross. "Well sweetie
then you'll have to find a way to get moved before Mitch
leaves." He tells her. "Or you can just come home, It's your
call." He says squeezing the can, tossing it into the trash
can close to the kitchen. "Daddy I'm not coming home
there's no room for me and the kids here, is there?" "No,
you belong at home with your husband, we are retired.
Unless you are in some trouble and it's a holiday, sweetie
we really love our peace, we are enjoying each other and
the privacy we have now, all those years with you and your
siblings, no sweetie there's no turning back for us, I mean
don't get me wrong we love for you to visit but staying, no,
no, no." He said shaking his head. "I know dad I won't
impose; it must have been hard all those years raising us."
Sara said looking at all the photos on the wall, she was one
of eight children. Mom and dad had five boys and three
girls they were all grown and doing well all over the
country her brothers all served in the military two in the air
force, three in the navy they all married and had children of
their own as well.

Her mom and dad were very proud. While mom was
still in the kitchen with the children, Sara finished her tea
with dad. She went into her old room where her and the
children would be sleeping that night. "Mom where is the
bedding for this bed in here?" She yelled out. "In the
cabinet dear right by the bathroom where I always keep
them," she tells her. "Thank you, mom!" She started
making the bed for the children. Mitchell called her over
and over she just couldn't talk to him now. She was so
afraid of going back home. Mitchell wasn't afraid of home
because he ignored all of what he saw there, even the
feathers that came from Williams mouth that day. How

could he have ignored that? She wondered while she made the bed. He was leaving soon what would she be left to do but be afraid, wandering around town like a crazy woman scared to go home and face the ghost. She shook her head, it sounds so crazy just thinking about it, she thought as she cleaned around in the room. The kids came into the room stuffed from grandma's cooking. They were so tired from the drive. Sara got them all into their pajamas and put them in her old bed. She laid next to them until they fell off to sleep. She kissed Tessa on her forehead with a sigh of relief. She took her phone from the dresser quietly walking out of the door, leaving it cracked so that she could hear them. She would go out into the living room area with mom and dad talk a little more, then she'll call Mitchell just to let him know that they were safe. She was still very angry at Mitchell for not taking action. She really couldn't explain her anger because it really wasn't Mitchell's fault at all it was whatever happened in that house before them. Maybe her dad was right, she thought as she sat down on the floor next to him.

"Daddy maybe you're right, I should investigate what happened there before we got there, maybe I will." She tells him grabbing her cup from the table. "Ouch it's hot!" She said almost dropping the cup. "Oh yeah I warmed the cup for you sweetie, I figured you'd come back for it." Mom said smiling. "You are the only person I know who takes all day to drink one cup of coffee or tea, you haven't changed dear." Her mother says to her sipping her tea. "Mom I always finish." She said giggling. "It's good to see you sweetie, I'm so glad I can enjoy my grandbabies." She turned to the television. "So, what's this I hear you're fighting with ghost in your house?" She asked her. "Dad? Why'd you tell her?" She said putting her cup down again.

"Do you really think I gave it away, sweetie your mom can hear a good story a mile away, her hearing is like dog hearing, those ears catch everything you say, even when you're not talking to her." Dad said laughing. "She's always been that way even while we were young." He says. "So, are you and the ghost friends or they're scary ghost?" She asked sarcastically. "Mom we are definitely not friends and of course they are scary mom it's not a joke." She took her cup up from the table and went out onto the porch to drink her tea and to call Mitchell. There was a swing on the porch overlooking the lake across from her parent's home. There were trees all around, you could hear the crickets, you could see the night bugs flying around the porch peacefully minding their own business. She sat down in the swing sipping her tea looking at the night sky.

After taking a few sips of tea from her cup she put the cup down, grabbing her phone staring at it for a while before calling Mitchell. It was late maybe he wouldn't pick up. She thought as she dialed him up. "Hello Sara." He said immediately. "Hi Mitch, how are you?" She asked him. "Baby come home what's wrong, why are you at your parent's?" He asked her. "Mitch, you know why." She told him. "No Sara we always said if we had something going on we would never do this once we were married, we'd take care of things ourselves remember?" He said. "I know Mitch, but this is different, this is about the family and it's getting very dangerous." She tells him. "Yes, I know you think it is but honey these are ghosts we're talking about, I don't want to be the crazy family in the neighborhood let's just sit down and figure this out, come home please baby." "I don't know Mitchell; can we talk about moving into a different house?" She asked. "Yes, baby but you know I will be leaving soon, your safety is most important to me especially while I'm away, baby I miss you." He tells her. "I miss you too Mitch, I will just stay the weekend we'll be home Sunday evening." She tells him. "Okay good baby, how are my babies doing? I miss them." He tells her. "They're being spoiled up here, you know mom's going to feed them everything she can find in the kitchen and cookie them up too," she said laughing. They went on talking through the night until Sara got tired. "I love you baby." Mitchell said hanging up the phone.

Sara stood up holding her cup and her phone in one hand using her other hand to open the door. As she got up to open the door, she glanced to take one look at the night sky and the lake, she saw standing behind the trees five tall figures. They peeped out from behind the trees. There were Fireflies flying all around the trees. She stepped back from the door taking a step forward to get a closer look, then out of the shadows near the trees came a tall shadow over the lake, a tall man with a cowboy hat on. She grabbed onto the door handle quickly going inside, shutting the door behind her. She looked from the window; the men were still lurking behind the trees. The shadow was now at the bottom of the stairs. She stared out at it, what the hell? She thought as she stood there watching the men staring back at the house. What did they want from her family she thought? She closed the window and went to the kitchen to put away her glass then up to the bedroom to lay with the children. When she went to the room, she begins taking off her clothing to get into her pajamas. She turned to her old dresser drawer to go looking for an old T- shirt she knew she had one in there, her mom never threw anything away. As she scrambled through the drawer quietly, she noticed a shadow at the window. She grabbed a shirt from the drawer, put it on over her head and ran to the window to see who was there. When she peeked out, she saw a figure with a cowboy hat walking away from the porch, she shut the curtain quickly, covering her mouth shaking her head. They followed her home, she thought as she sat down next to the children on the bed. She counted heads knowing that they were there. She'd left the kids alone sleeping, she couldn't trust that they wouldn't try to hurt them while they were there. She sat up all night watching them sleep and watching the window.

When morning came, she woke up with her head pressed to the window. She snatched her head up shifting her neck too quickly, she was in pain. She rubbed her neck looking down at the bed, the children were gone, she didn't hear them anywhere in the house. She picked her phone up from the floor looking at the time it was only 10:20am mom would be cooking in the kitchen she thought. Where were they, she thought leaving the room quickly. She walked out into the living room. "Dad! Mom!" She yelled out. "Hey kids where are you guys?" She yelled out walking toward the kitchen. She went to the backyard, maybe they were out gardening with her parents she thought. They weren't out at the garden, she walked around from the back to the front looking for them. As she approached the front end of the side of the house, she could hear the children laughing with her mom and dad. "Hey mom!" William yelled out at her as she approached the front of the house near the lake. William was playing football with her dad while her mom played with Jonah and Tessa near the lakebed. "Hey sweetie, I left you breakfast on the counter in the kitchen"! Her mom yelled out to her. "Thanks mom but I'm not hungry!" She said going to the front steps sitting down. She watched from the stairs the kids played with her parents by the lake. William walked over to her sitting next to her sweating. "Mom grandpa is wearing me out, how old is he again?" William asked. Sara laughed pushing his hair back from his face. "You're so cute, you know I can't tell you his age he'll never forgive me." She said, "He likes playing the younger men he stays fit that way." She said laughing. "You have to keep playing with him he loves it." She tells him.

"I'm tired mom I can't, look at him he's got too much energy mom." William said smiling, her father came running over with Jonah now on his back. "Hey what happened son you can't hang with an old man huh?" He says to William. "Yes, grandpa you're too much, I just can't hang." He said laughing. "Grandpa understands son, but I want you to come back out here to spend time with me and grandma this summer, we can work out together I can whip you into shape." He said bouncing Jonah around on his back. Just as they were sitting talking Sara noticed her mom frantically racing down the to the edge of the lakebed looking around, she even went into the cold lake water. "Mom! Is everything okay!" She yelled. "Susan what's wrong!" Her father shouted out. "I can't find her!" "What mom!" Sara said running over to the lake. "Boy's stay here don't move!" Her father said dropping Jonah to his feet from his back. "Stay here!" They both ran over to where mom was. Dad went into the lake and began swimming around "Tessa! Tessa! Sara yelled out "Mom where was she last?" Sara yelled out. "I watched her run, she wanted to look at the flowers, I turned around to pick up my shoes to run behind her and she was gone!" Her mom said crying. Everyone was crying and looking around for Tessa. Her dad was in the water swimming around looking for her while Sara searched around the trees near the wooded area.

"Tessa! Tessa! Tess baby where are you!" Sara screamed out, "Baby girl where are you!" She yelled out. She kept going deeper into the wooded area then came out. When she got to the edge of the property, she turned around to go back. "Any luck?" Her father screamed out to her. "No dad please keep searching!" She screamed out. "Sara! Any luck?" he screamed out again." "No dad!" She screamed out louder. She looked again throughout the trees in the wooded areas. Sara sobbed and sobbed as she walked around searching for Tessa until the sun begin to go down while her parents called their neighbors and the sheriff department to come out to help search. Soon the sun had faded, while they searched the lake with the sheriff department and the boys went inside with her mom to call Mitchell, Sara decided to search again at the edge of the property. While walking back she saw in the darkness near the trees the pioneer woman from the house standing with the cowboy holding baby Tessa in her arms. She began to run toward them as fast as she could. "Tessa! Tessa!" She ran screaming Tessa's name. The Sheriff saw that she was frantic. He stopped the search in the lake, everyone was wet running behind her. When she got to the tree the pioneer woman sat Tessa down on the ground as she'd done before at the house and turned away. As she walked away, she yelled out to Sara, "Don't leave your baby alone!" The cowboy grabbed her by the arm walking her into the woods where they faded away. Sara grabbed Tessa from the ground holding her as tight as she could. Her mom and the boys, her dad and the Sheriff all ran to her hugging her and holding on to one another. "Where was she?" Her dad asked, "Where'd you find her?" He asked again. Sara looked at him with tears in her eyes. "Dad, they had her." She told him walking toward the house.

Where We Go, They Will Follow

Sara went into her parent's home that night unable to explain to the Sheriff what she meant by they had her when asked where Tessa was, she told her mom that she was just afraid, she didn't know what she was saying at the time. She called Mitchell telling him not to worry, that Tessa had wondered off and she was fine. She was so scared, the boys sat with her mom in the kitchen. She fed them dinner along with the neighbors and the Sheriff, everyone was happy that we found Tessa and that she was safe. Sara was still in a state of shock she couldn't believe that they had Tessa in the woods. She couldn't believe that they were in Oregon, that they followed her to her parent's home. This meant that they weren't just ordinary ghost they want something from her family, they are looking for something she thought, but what can it be? She thought while she sat there listening to her dad talk to the Sheriff about all his medals around the house. The Sheriff was a retired Airman as well, they compared medals and stories for hours. Sara held Tessa close until she fell off to sleep. "Mom, do you think I can have a cup of tea please?" She yelled out to her. "Of course, dear." Her mom yelled out to her. She was entertaining the boys, baking cookies they were enjoying her so much. Sara almost hated the thought of taking them home the next day, but she'd promised Mitchell already that she'd be home.

When everyone left and it was quiet, her dad came over to the living room where she was. He rubbed her head

"Hey you!" He said tapping her on the nose. "How are you doing?" He asked. "I know today was awful, I don't know what we would have done if we didn't find her, thank god we found her." He said shaking his head. "I don't think your mother would have been able to bare it." He said. "I know daddy, but we found her." Sara said. "Yes, did you call Mitchell?" He asked. "Yes, I called him, he's happy we'll be back tomorrow," she tells her dad. "So, you're okay now sweetie, you just do what I told you, tell good old Mitchell to get you and the kids some other place before he leaves and you should be okay, some of those old places have bad memories left in them." He tells her rubbing her head getting up from his chair. "And this summer William needs to come hangout with his grandparents, don't forget us while we can still do, we're still quite the fit team." He said flexing his muscles smiling at Sara. She went to bed holding Tessa on her chest. She was so afraid to lay her down on the bed, she watched the boys all night. When the sun began to rise, she got up with Tessa in her arms. She started packing the backpack she came with and her purse to leave, she was very nervous for the journey home, but she knew she had to get back to Mitchell.

She went into the kitchen where her mom and dad were sitting having breakfast. "Are the children up dear, I've made them breakfast." Her mom says to her. "Not yet mom, just me and Tessa." She said sitting Tessa on her mother's lap. "You know Sara you're going to make her rotten like that, carrying her around on your hip wherever you go, how will she ever learn to do things on her own?" Her mother said to her getting up to place Tessa in an old wooden highchair she'd keep in the kitchen for her grandbabies. "No mom she'll be okay, after what happened yesterday, I just want to hold on to her, is that okay?" Sara said to her mom. "Sure, dear just be careful with that, she doesn't need you holding on to her all day long, it'll ruin her, she won't know how to socialize with other children her age or anything, but she's your baby you do what you want." Her mother said feeding baby Tessa cereal from a spoon. Sara's dad looked at her mother crossed with his reading glasses hanging from his face. "Well, it was sure nice seeing you and the children, next time you should give us a heads up and we'll have more for them to do and the holiday season's approaching, I hope you'll be coming back especially if Mitch will be gone for the holidays." He tells her looking up at her. "Oh yes daddy I will be back, I don't know if it'll be for the holidays though this was quite a drive for me." Sara tells him.

She left soon after the children ate breakfast, she was so exhausted still from what happened the day before she only stopped a few times on the road for gas and for the children to get snacks and pee. She held onto Tessa tight even using the restroom with her on her lap afraid to leave any of them anywhere. She took them all into the stalls with her when they stopped.

She was so nervous about going home but she needed to see Mitch. She needed to tell him the truth and make him understand now she knows that it doesn't matter where they go these ghostly things are following her and the children. Just as she was about five miles away from home, she saw the Indians running alongside her car, she saw the cowboys and the pioneer woman waving at her from the side of the road. She tried her best to ignore what she was seeing. Maybe I'm delusional she thought, rolling the window down to catch the fresh air to her face. Maybe I'm just too tired, I'm not thinking straight and I'm not seeing straight, two more miles and I will be home. She went a little faster on the highway just to make up a little time. She wanted to get home before the sun went down. She could tell she was losing time when the air gotten colder, and the sky turned red. She rolled the window up when she saw the California city limits sign. Thank God she thought, I am only a mile out from home. She was about a block away from the housing area, right at the turn where there's a dead-end street on the left side of the housing complex is a little church. She'd never notice the church before, but it was there. She slowed down to look at it, old and small. As she slowed, she saw the pioneer woman standing around the church waving at her.

She turned her head quickly driving down the road to her house, the church was literally two blocks away one right, one block and a left and she was home in the cul-de-sac where she lived. When she pulled up it was dark out. Mitchell just happened to be in the garage fixing on an old bike that he'd had for years. As they pulled up, he walked over to the car with his dirty rag in his hand. "Hey family welcome home." He said with a smile, as he began to grab the children out of the car helping Sara, he took her backpack giving her a long kiss. "Hello, I'm so glad you're home baby, I have a surprise for you later." He said, rubbing his body against hers. "Mitch not in front of the children!" Sara said with a smile, holding Tessa in her arms. "Hey dad, grandpa said I can go back for the summer." William told him. "Yes, I heard all about that, your grandpa is quite the guy, isn't he?" He responded with a nod. "I'm so glad you're home." He says to Sara as they walked into the house through the side door of the garage. When they went inside, William stood still in the doorway, it was as if he saw someone standing in front of him. "Son what's wrong?" Mitchell asked him. He didn't respond to him, looking straight ahead Jonah ran to the stairwell. "Hi Shadow!" He said with excitement in his eyes. "Look daddy Shadows here!" he said pointing up at the stairwell. Mitchell went over to him grabbed him from his feet. "No son Shadows not here he's not!" Mitchell said, "He's not real okay son."

"You have to stop playing with shadow, he's not really there, son." He tells Jonah. William still stood there waiting in the doorway. He could hear the hand drum; it would get loud then low; he couldn't move until now. He'd forgotten about the little hand drum. "William!" Sara shouted. "William! Hey! snap out of it!" Sara said loudly. "William!" She placed her purse down onto the table in the living room. She went over to William clutching baby Tessa to her hip. "Hey!" She said shaking his arm. "What's wrong with you?" Sara said holding his arm. William stood still looking straight, she snapped her fingers in front of his face. "Hey son!" Mitchell said loudly getting into his face. "Huh dad?" William responded. "What's wrong with you?" Mitchell asked him. "I hear it, don't you guys hear it?" He asked them, walking all around the room, looking behind the couches and underneath the tables and in the cabinets. "You guys don't hear it! He yelled going into the garage dropping the backpack from his shoulder that he carried in from the car. "William what do you hear, what are you looking for?" Mitchell asked him. By then William was already inside the garage pulling things form the boxes, grabbing things from the shelf. "Dad, it has to be here don't you hear it?" He yelled out. "Don't you hear the drum?" He yelled shaking one of the boxes holding it upside down. "No son I don't hear anything." Mitchell said to him. "Come inside now, come in!" He yelled in a very stern voice. "No dad you don't understand I lost something that Sabien gave me as a gift. It was something very important, he told me never to lose it or give it away!" He yelled out as his dad begin to tug onto his shirt pulling him inside.

"Son, listen I don't care what you lost, you're acting crazy, now come inside!" We will figure this out later." He yelled out pulling him inside the house. "Mitchell what's he talking about?" Sara asked standing in the doorway waiting for him to get inside. "He's talking about some drum he's hearing, something about the neighbor kid Sabien gave him a drum set or something." Mitchell tells her rubbing his head shaking it, looking over at William who was still looking around the room for the drum. "Wait William who gave you a drum set?" Sara asked. "It's not a drum set mom it is a little hand drum and someone's playing with it right now, I hear it don't you guys hear it?" He tells her looking around the room. "Okay William just relax, sit down on the couch I will help you find it I promise, when did he give it to you?" She asked handing Tessa to Mitchell. "Hold on to her do not let her out of your sight." She tells him placing her in his lap. "William what does it look like?" She asked him looking around the house. "It's a hand drum mom, it looks colorful, it has a handle on it and a lot of colors on it and there's feathers on the ends of the strings tied to it with beads to make the drum sounds." He tells her covering his ears, the drums were beating louder. "William what's wrong?" Sara asked going over to him. He kept his hand over his ears closing his eyes, shaking his head now. When he closed his eyes, he could see the Indians dancing around a fire and chanting a song. They were looking at him with anger in their eyes, their faces colored white and red and black, their feathered headbands covered their heads with white and brown feathers this time. "No! No! No!" William screamed, "No!" The drums were so loud in his ears he couldn't hear anything. His mom raced around the house looking everywhere. William screamed out. "Daddy Help Me!" When he opened his eyes, the cowboy was standing in front of him staring him in the face.

He tipped his hat to him, the drums in his ears went low "Find the drum boy." He said to him breathing into is face. William covered his eyes, crawled up onto the couch into a fetal position with his knees to his face and his hands over his head. He began to rock back and forth shaking like a leaf. "William!" Sara said trying to pull his hand from his head. "What's wrong with you? What's going on? Talk to me son!" She said, now curling her arm around him holding him crying. "Mom, I have to find that drum." He said in a muffled whisper.

They Just Become Dangerous

William stayed on the couch that night crying as Sara held him. She cried along with him. Mitchell held onto Tessa sitting across from them while Jonah played around the room. Nothing seemed to be bothering Jonah at all. Sara began to ask William what he meant when he said he had to find the drum, did someone tell him that? William shook his head yes. "Well tells us son, who told you to find it?" She asked him. "The cowboy, mom the cowboy got into my face and told me to find it!" He said still muffled but yelling with his head to his knees. "I see this drum is what he wants, why?" Sara asked, "I don't know mom, Sabien gave me the drum as a going away present, he didn't say that it belonged to someone else." He tells her. "Hmm, okay son I will call Sabien's mom tomorrow to ask about the drum." "No mom, you can't call her! Sabien said I couldn't tell them I had it. I wasn't supposed to tell anyone." He tells her peeking his eyes out from in between his legs. "Why not where did he get the drum from?" He asked him. William shook his head. "I don't know mom, I just know he told me I couldn't tell anyone," he said putting his head back down. Jonah came over to him, put his little hand on his head ruffling his hair. "Don't worry William, Shadow won't hurt you, he's my friend." He said running off again with his little car in his hand. "Okay I know you don't want me to ask Sabien's mother but William that drum could be the reason for all this funky stuff happening around here." Sara said standing to her feet, going over to Mitchell to grab Tessa. "I mean where did it come from?" She said shaking her head.

"Mom, you don't believe that do you? It's just a small hand drum it's not a witch's wand or anything, it's a fun hand drum it doesn't have any powers or anything." He tells her. "You don't know that William, isn't Sabien a Native American Indian? She asked him. "Didn't the mom once live on the reservation?" "Yes, mom but what does that mean? He's still an American!" He said standing to his feet running up to his room. "Mom, I can't believe you think he'd give me something to curse us with! I can't believe you!" He stormed off to his room. Sara sat down beside Mitchell. "Baby you did sound a little racist just then." "No Mitchell you know that I am the last person to say or think anything like that but I know that on the reservation some of the Native Americans have rituals and they have sacred symbols and tools that they use in some rituals, you know that they do, it's usually nothing evil though Mitchell but it's sacred not to be touched, we have to find out about that drum Mitchell she said with tears in her eyes. "What if he gave him something he wasn't supposed to give him, what if that's the reason they are here?" She said to Mitchell. "We have to find out." Mitchell stood up next to her. "You're right, I don't believe in those sorts of things, but this is real, I've seen it." He said walking to the stairs. "I say call the mom see where that drum came from, so we can do what we can to get it back to them maybe then all this madness will stop." He said going up the stairs. Sara had been driving all day, she was exhausted, she thought maybe after she gets Tessa to bed, she could take a hot shower. She'd be able to sleep especially since Mitchell was home tonight. She got up from the couch and turned the television off clutching Tessa to her hip. She turned to go up to bed. When she turned the light off in the den area the television came back on. Sara walked back over to the television, grabbed the remote from the table turning it off again. When she walked back to the stairs it came right back on. This time the volume was turning up louder and louder. She held the remote to the TV, pushing the volume button as hard as she could to turn it down, but it wouldn't budge. Soon Mitchell came running down the stairs. "Sara what's going on?" He yelled out. "It won't budge it won't turn down." She said holding the remote to the television. Mitchell took the remote trying to turn it down himself, it still wouldn't budge. He went over to the TV using the buttons on the television but still it wouldn't budge. He reached behind the television snatching the cord from the wall, the television went off. "There that took care of that." He said taking Tessa from Sara's arms. "Let's go get some rest baby it's late." Sara followed behind him turning the light off behind her, as they walked up the stairs the lights flashed on and off on and off, Mitchell looked back at Sara. "Just leave it alone, we ignore it, it's not really happening," he said headed to the top of the stairwell. "I don't think most people understand, sometimes you just have to ignore stuff like that." Sara walked up behind him grabbing onto his pants. She kept looking back, watching, hoping that nothing else happened to them on the way up.

When they got to the bedroom Mitchell held Tessa to his chest. "Baby I'm going to put her to sleep while you shower, go ahead I know you're exhausted, go ahead take your shower baby, don't worry enjoy it or better yet why don't you soak in the tub baby." I may join you if she goes down soon." He tells her. "No Mitchell don't leave her alone." She tells him while she goes into the master bath to start her bath water. She spreads bath salts all into the water. She begins to undress wrapping herself in her robe, sliding her feet into her slippers. She walks down the hall to check on the boys before she goes to bed. She goes to William's room first the door was cracked open the room was dim with just the light from the closet. She peeked inside. William was sleeping soundly, she went to the closet to shut the door, William popped up. "No mom I like to sleep with it on, please leave it." He said. "Okay son no problem, good night then." She tells him, blowing him a kiss and waving good night. She headed back down the hall toward Jonah's room the door was closed shut. She opened it slowly trying not to wake him, the room was pitch black. She reached over to switch on the light, dimming it slowly so that she didn't wake him. Jonah had a night light on the table that he'd use every night, but it wasn't on. She went over to it and switched it on, only to find that Jonah wasn't in his bed, she tried not to panic. She looked underneath the bed but no Jonah, then she heard in a whisper. "Shh! Over here." From the closet, she was being watched by Jonah. "Honey why are you shushing me?" She asked him while opening the closet door. Jonah shook his head and shrugged his shoulders. "Okay you know it's bedtime, you can't stay up playing to late sweetie." She said kissing him on the cheek laying him in bed.

"I know mommy." He said yawning. "You know huh, well what's keeping you up so late sweetie?" She asked him. Jonah started to say his friend, but he caught himself, covering his mouth shaking his head. Sara moved his hand from his mouth. What's wrong, why can't you tell me what you were up to?" "Daddy says I can't play with my friends anymore." Just when he said that the closet light went off and the light in the room dimmed to its darkest level, and the light on Jonah's nightstand blinked on and off. Sara kissed Jonah on the forehead and reached for the light, turning it off hoping it would stay off. "Mommy's just going to leave the light dim for you okay baby?" She said walking toward the door to go get into her bath. She left Jonah's door open so she could hear him. "Now remember baby no more playing tonight okay, love you." She said walking away. "Love you more mommy, good night." He said in his sweet five year old voice. When she got back into her room Mitchell had put Tessa in her own bed. He was waiting for Sara in the tub. Sara was reluctant to leave Tessa in her own bedroom, although it was close. Every time she left Tessa the pioneer woman would come for her. Mitchell convinced her that she had to relax. He had soft music playing and the lights dimmed. "Come on baby get in here with me." He tells her. "I don't know." Sara said holding onto her robe. "The kids are alone in their rooms I just don't want to leave Tessa in there alone." She tells him standing over the bathtub holding onto the belt of her robe. "Okay then, take this bath with me relax a little and then you can go and get Tessa, but right now baby I need you too." He said standing up dripping wet reaching for her, pulling her into him close enough to kiss her. He removed her robe for her, throwing it to the floor grabbing her, standing her up near him. He began to kiss her all over. "I missed you baby; I need you right now." He whispers in her ear.

"I miss you too Mitch." They made love in the bathtub. When they were done, they sat in the tub. Mitch held onto Sara for a few before she began to get nervous, he kissed her neck off and on. "Just relax baby, just relax." He said moving her hair from her face. "I love you so much Sara, when will you give me my other baby?" "No not again Mitch, not now, relax remember?" She said sitting up from his chest looking back at him. Just when she looked back at

him the door opened wide, the light turned on bright, then the bathroom went dark. "Don't move."
Mitchell told her. "I don't want you to slip and fall." He stood up holding onto the wall, then the shower curtain stepping out of the tub leaving Sara there waiting. He went over to the light to turn it back on. Sara leaned back in the tub beginning to sob loudly. "Mitchell, I hate this!" She said crying, holding her head down. When she lifted her head in the darkness, she saw a face staring down at her moving its head from left to right. She jumped up as fast as she could. "Mitchell!" She screamed jumping out of the bathtub hitting her feet on the edge. "Mitchell!" Mitchell was still trying to turn the light switch on it wouldn't budge to switch on. Sara grabbed onto Mitchell's arm, they walked out of the bathroom naked. Mitchell grabbed his pants from the stool near the door and put them on quickly. He went over to the light switch in the bedroom, switching it on. "Sara what happened, what did you see?" He asked her. "I don't know what it was." She told him sobbing. "It was just a face staring at me moving his head from left to right, it was scary!" She grabbed her other robe off the door putting it on. "Baby it's okay, I'm going to check on the kids just go lay down okay." He tells her. "I promise everything will be okay." He tells her walking out of the room, it felt like the temperature dropped very low in the house, it was freezing. Mitchell wrapped his arms around his back, holding himself. As he walked away Sara grabbed the cover from the bed, wrapping it around herself, she could hear Mitchell walking all around checking on the kids. "Sara!" He yelled out. "Sara!" He yelled again. "Yes!" She called out to him. "I can't find Tessa!" Sara jumped to her feet, running from the bedroom down the hall to Tessa's room. "What! What do you mean?" She

yelled out. "See I told you, we can't leave her alone Mitchell! I told you!" She said running around the house. While she ran around downstairs Mitchell was looking everywhere upstairs. They called out to her over and over Mitchell woke the boys up. "Where's your sister did you see her?" He asked William. "Dad! What do you mean? I was sleeping how could I see her?" William said laying back down onto his pillow. "No William get up! Help us look for your sister." He said pulling the covers from William's bed. He sat up straight in bed then crawled out slowly. "Come on!" Mitchell yelled out to him running toward Jonah's room. By then Sara was already back up. She grabbed Jonah from bed. As she turned to take him from the room the door shut in her face hard, hard enough that his pictures fell from the wall and his desk and nightstand shook. "Open this door now!" She yelled "Now I said!" She kicked the door holding on to Jonah. "Now!" She yelled again.

Jonah woke up looking at the door, he kept looking at the closet door. "Open this door you motherfucker!!" Sara screamed, kicking the door with her bare feet. "Let me out of here!" She screamed. Jonah stared over at the closet door clutching onto her neck very tightly, then he whispered. "Don't cry please." He said with tears rolling down his little cheeks. Sara reached to open the door with her hand, it opened before she could grab the nob. She ran out to the hallway, then to her room. "Mitchell!" She yelled all through the hall. "Mitchell, I have Jonah do you have William?" She yelled going into her room she was still holding onto Jonah sobbing. She carried him over to the bed placing him on top when she noticed Tessa was laying underneath the sheets. She snatched the sheet quickly grabbing Tessa up into her arms. "Baby how'd you get there?" She asked, sobbing, kissing Tessa's face. "How did you get in here?" She sobbed holding her. "Mitchell! Mitchell! I got her she's here!" She yelled out sobbing. Mitchell came up the stairs running with William trailing behind, him jumping onto the bed. "Where was she?" He asked holding onto them both. "She was in the bed, in our bed underneath the sheets." She tells him. "When did she get there?" Mitchell asked, "I don't know," she tells him shaking her head. William sat on the bed crying. "Mom I'm so sorry I may have brought something here and cursed us." He said sobbing. "No son you didn't." Mitchell told him. "You don't know what that thing was." He tells him rubbing his head. "It's okay son this will be over soon." He tells him. "We will all sleep in here together until it's over." Mitchell tells them all, getting the blanket from the floor. "The bed's big enough." He said shaking the blanket out. They all laid down, the kids in the middle, Sara on one side Mitchell on the other. They left the light on in the room, cuddle up together in the bed. Sara and Mitchell held their hands over the children, clutching them together watching them fall off to sleep. "How did she get in the bed?" Mitchell sill questioned. "It was Shadow daddy! He put her in bed for mommy, he's my friend." Jonah said with his little eyes closed shut.

Beating Drum

Night after night they slept together as a family in one bed, in one room. Sara would bathe then bathe the children while she stayed close by leaving the door cracked, while William showered or used the bathroom. There were so many things happening every day and every night. Mitchell would try keeping things normal; however, Sara would stretch her resources all day not bothering her neighbors anymore but hanging out at the military rec center. She'd get the boys from the bus every day, taking them for swimming lessons at the rec center while her and baby Tessa watched. She would teach Tessa to swim as well. Sara had written a letter to the family back in their old housing community hoping to find out about the drum that was given to William, they hadn't contacted her. It had been a week already when Mitchell came home to tell Sara that he would be deploying in a month. "I will have to be out for 9 months this time baby; I've already put us on the list to move." He told her. "But it could take forever for them to place us here in the same complex, what do I do if they don't move us?" Sara asked Mitchell. "Baby we can't keep living in fear, we have to find a way to deal with it, have you been able to reach his friends mother at all?" He asked her. She shook her head no.

"I hope they are still there in New York, what if they've been relocated and have a different phone number Mitchell?" She said looking around the room for her phone.

Tessa was sitting on the floor in front of her looking up holding her phone in her small hand.

"What about the housing welcome book that was given to us when we moved in, there should be some numbers to call on their list to find other military wives if need be right?" "You're right, I could probably reach out to the ombudsman on the ship her husband was last on." Sara said grabbing Tessa from the floor taking her phone, heading to the garage to go through her old contact list for the last command ship her husband was on with the neighbor. "While you do that, I will make us some dinner baby." Mitchell said, kissing her on the forehead, walking toward the kitchen. "Boys come in and help me!" He yelled out to the boys who were playing in the backyard with the neighbor kids. William opened the door just a little to peek his head in. "Dad I just want to play for a few more minutes, please dad, can I?" He asked him with excitement on his face. "Okay well keep a close eye out for your brother." He told him. "Keep him with you at all times." William slammed the door so hard that it snapped back leaving it cracked opened just a little. Mitchell looked out, watching William run back over to his friends as they threw a football toward him, he jumped into the air catching it throwing it back. Jonah stayed close; William nudged him to stand back so that he wouldn't get hurt. As Mitchel watched on only turning his back to get food from the refrigerator maintaining a close watch on the boys he cooked as fast as he could. The sun began to set Mitchell looked out at the boys. "Hey, can you set the table?" He asked Sara as she walked into the kitchen with Tessa on her hip.

"Sure," she said placing Tessa into her highchair securing her in. "Where are the boys?" She asked Mitchell. Just as he begins to ask, William came running into the house opening the slide in door wide as if he needed lots of space to get inside. Jonah followed right behind him. "Okay boys let's get washed up dinner's ready!" Mitchell tells them pointing to the rest room. They both ran to the bathroom. Sara followed closely behind them. "Sara they'll be okay baby I think you can let them go alone." Mitchell yells out to her. "No, I will watch them!" She said, walking behind them. "Me first!" Jonah screamed out trying to run ahead of William, almost tripping over his feet. "No, I really must go, you wait!" William said to Jonah shoving him away from the doorway. Jonah crossed his arms at the door glaring at him. "You always get to go first it's just not fair!" He said looking up at Sara. "Oh, don't be mad sweetie he'll be quick," she tells him, rubbing his shoulder. William shut the door leaving it slightly opened so that his mom could hear him. "Hurry, and make sure you wash your hands." Sara tells him, holding Jonah's shoulders. "Mom I'm going as fast as I can." He said walking over to the sink to wash his hands looking at the mirror while he soaped up his hands slowly washing them. "Come on!" Jonah said yelling. It looked as if someone pushed him out of the way of the door. "Okay I'm coming." William said, shutting the water off. The lights went off in the bathroom, the door slammed shut as soon as William reached for the towel on the wall to dry his hands.

"Mom!" He yelled. "Mom! Help me! I can't see in here!" He yelled. He starts to hear the hand drum shaking and beating loudly, he felt someone standing in front of him and behind him. He could hear them breathing while the drum played loudly. "Mom!" He yelled reaching out for the doorknob. "William pull it open!" His mom screamed out to him. She pushed and kicked, screaming for William to open the door. "William open up!" She yelled listening to him scream out for her. "I can't mom it won't budge!" He yelled out. "Mitchell come help me please!" Sara screamed out crying. Jonah stood back watching, looking up into the air as if he was mesmerized by something ahead of him. "Jonah go sit with your sister!" Mitchell told him running over to her. "No Mitchell go back! Do not leave them alone!" She yelled. "I will get William out!" She yelled. "Please hand me a knife!" She screamed. "A knife?" Mitchell yelled back. "Yes, a big sharp knife!" She tells him, hurrying him with her hand gesture. "I will pry it open," She yelled. Mitchell went running toward the kitchen sink to grab a knife. "Mitchell hurry I don't hear him anymore he's not moving around!"

She said crying. "Sara go sit with the kids, I will get him out." Mitchell went to the bathroom door pushing Sara away to move to the kitchen with the little ones. She grabbed Jonah, pulling him into the kitchen standing close to Tessa by the slide in door. "William, do you hear me!" Mitchell shouted out. By this time William had covered his ears trying to keep himself from hearing the drum, his hands were to his ears, he cried in a soft whisper over and over; "Help me dad! Help me mom! Help me! Help me, help me."

He was so afraid, he could now feel the feathers being swept across his face, tickling his nose and his neck. He was still, with tears running down his cheeks. He couldn't respond to his mother or father as they yelled for him to answer him. Mitchell began to hit the door with his shoulder, holding and twisting the doorknob. "William!

William! Say something buddy, say anything!" He said to him slamming his shoulder into the door, kicking it as hard as he could with his foot to open it up, it wouldn't budge at all. Mitchell began to get so frustrated, he started to beat on the door as hard as he could. "Buddy listen, we're going to get you out of there don't worry!" He said leaving the door going to the garage. "Mitchell don't leave him!" Sara yelled out to him. "I have to go get something, hold on." He yelled, holding the garage door open. He ran out and came back in with an ax he began to hit the door with it as hard as he could, hitting the doorknob and the door. "Stand back William, stand back!" He yelled out hitting the door over and over. William stood still, eyes closed holding his hands to his ears, with his eyes filled with tears rolling down his face. He couldn't hear anything except for the muffled sound of the drums. He stood still, he could feel the feathers rubbing his forehead, neck and cheeks. He just couldn't open his eyes; he was so afraid of what he would see this time. He stood there crying, hoping that the door would open, and the light would come on soon. He could even feel the breath of the Indian men on his face, they were right in his face. He sighed taking deep short breaths and counting to himself, hoping the door would open all while Mitchell was hitting the door trying to get in. He hit the door as hard as he could with the ax. Sara and the kids stood back watching, the family was in tears.

Suddenly the drums stopped beating. William screamed out, "Daddy! Help me please!" With his ears still covered he opened his eyes to the darkness, staring right into his eyes was a Native American man with his face painted white. His eyes were red he pressed his nose to the tip of Williams nose, he yelled into his face. "We are broken!" The lights came on and the door opened wide, slamming against the wall making a small hole. Mitchell went in grabbing William by the arm, pulling him out holding him in his arms. "Son are you okay, are you hurt?" He asked William, looking him over. "No dad William said shaking his head. Mitchell walked him over to the kitchen table where Sara and the kids were waiting. Sara grabbed onto William. "Son are you okay?" She asked him, squeezing him tight. "I am okay mom, I'm hungry." He said sitting down at the table. "I don't want to talk about it mom, I just want to eat please." He said pushing his chair in close to the table. It was as if he'd had enough of the scary stuff. "Okay son." Mitchell said going over to the stove to grab the food he cooked earlier. "Everyone eat up then we'll head up to bed." He said to them placing the food on the table. "It's a hamburger surprise dish I created to eat when I'm deployed, and they want to feed me food I don't like." He sat down at the table with the family. They held hands; Sara prayed. "Bless our family tonight lord please keep us all safe from harm and please bless this food we are about to receive in Jesus' name." They all said Amen, lifted their heads and begin to grab the food, passing it around the table to one another. They could hear walking around upstairs. Mitchell looked up then down at the kids.

When dinner was over, they cleaned the kitchen together. No one really said a word. Mitchell was so upset at what was happening and Sara was sadden by the thought of having all the troubles of having to move somewhere else, relocating the kids again, it was going to be a very difficult thing to do without Mitchell. She wondered if she'd ever hear from Sabine's family, if she could just get them to tell her about the hand drum then maybe she'd be able to go on and not be bothered by these spiritual encounters. They all went upstairs to the bedroom to get ready for bed again.

They washed up together in the bathroom. Sara watched as they all got into their pajamas, helping the little ones while William went to the back of the closet alone to get dressed. "Mom can't we just go back to grandma's house?" He asked her, taking off his shirt. "I wish it was the simple William, I really do." She told him grabbing Tessa, leaving the closet. Mitchell turned the lights down in the house. They all got into bed. Mitchell slept with his leg hanging out of the covers every night with his foot dangling off the side of the bed to keep cool. "There are so many bodies in here." He would say to Sara holding her by the waist side pulling her close. Sara would just smile looking at the kids. Their days were intense each day. They'd spend most of their time watching the children closely, never leaving them alone in the house and while they were out of the house they'd stay out as long as they could. Sara dreaded going home, every day she grew more stressed and tired. The house would become unkempt from lack of her being there long enough to clean in the daytime. Mitchell began to worry more that Sara was becoming depressed, unable to care for the children properly while he was away at work.

On the days he worked late she'd take them out to eat and they'd sit outside until he came home. Some nights he wouldn't get in until 11pm at night. Sara would sit on the porch waiting for him she didn't have to, but she did in fear that she might have an encounter every day, especially weekdays. She would stay in front watching the children play and when they were done, she'd sit out there with snacks to feed them if they began to get hungry. One day while sitting outside Jonah played around on the front lawn as if he was being chased by someone. He was laughing so hard running and falling to the ground as if he was really being chased. He ran over to Sara, she was sitting on the chair in front of the door on the porch. He tapped her on the leg. "Mommy! Mommy!" He said pointing over at the man across the street mowing his lawn. "Mr. Bennett is going to die today." He said pointing at the man across the street the man was mowing his lawn sweating a lot wiping his forehead over and over with a rag. Sara looked at Jonah. "Hey, don't say things like that Jonah, he'll be fine." She told him looking over confused about why he'd say a thing like that. "No mommy, he will die today." "Hey Jonah stop that, stop talking like that." She tells him again shooing him to go play. "Go on go play!" She tells him. "Okay mom but Shadow says the man will die today." He said looking over at the man while he mowed his lawn. Sara stood to her feet with her hand to her hip clutching Tessa to her other hip. The sound of the name Shadow now scared her. She knew that if Jonah said it that Shadow was surely around. "Come on Jonah were taking a ride." She tells him waving him to come to the porch. "Aww man mom, no!" I don't want to go for another ride. I just want to stay home and play with Shadow." He tells her. "No son we have to go now, where's your brother?" She asked him.

"How should I know?" He said moping around her. "Maybe he ran away, we don't ever get to have any fun!" He tells her with his head down. "We will have fun soon enough." She tells him, rubbing his little head. "William!" She screamed out. "William!" William came running down the street with a few friends running behind him. "Hey mom what's going on?" He asked Sara. "We have to go for a ride." She tells him standing in front of them. "I don't want to go mom, come on can't we just stay around here for a few? The sun will be going down soon, and we were going to play hide and seek!" He tells her looking at his friends. "Play hide and seek another day." She tells him walking toward the car. "Mom can we please stay and play with our friends?" He asked. "I promise I won't play with Shadow anymore!" Jonah said looking up at her. "He has to go see Mr. Bennett anyway." He tells her pointing across the street. By then Mr. Bennett was inside, leaving his lawn mower out in front of his house. Just as she started to put Tessa into the car, Barbra walked over to her. "Going somewhere?" She asked her, holding the car door open. "You never come by to see me anymore since the cat incident, are you okay?" She asked her standing close to the car door staring over at Tessa. "My goodness you're getting to be a very big girl!" She said smiling down at Tessa. "Oh no, I'm well, I just thought you needed a little space after that, I know losing a pet is like losing a family member, so I just wanted to give you a little space." She said to her standing back looking around for Jonah. "Oh, he ran over there to play with the boys over there." She tells her, pointing at the mailboxes near the fence. "So why don't you stick around sweetie I'm doing much better." She tells her. "The cats may have gotten sick off the rat poison I had been leaving out to catch some little mice I was chasing around here." She told her pulling a cigarette from her shorts. "Sweetie, you look terrible are you sure you're doing okay over here?" She asked her placing the cigarette onto her lips.

"I'm okay." Sara told her, grabbing Tessa from her car seat. "I guess we will just stick around until daddy gets here." She tells her, walking over to the porch to sit down. "I bet you've been having a lot of sleepless nights honey, I heard about your husband having to be deployed soon." She said moving her hair from her face looking at Sara with the cigarette hanging from her lip. She had a very strong Kentucky accent, very country. "No, I'm just not use to being here in this way." She tells her. "Well honey it gets better I'm telling you; my husband and I have been there, you look like you're really having a hard time, he will come back you know he won't be gone forever." She tells her taking the cigarette from her lip. "No that's not it." Sara tells her scooting around in her chair placing it in front of Barbra on the porch. "Barbra there's been some things going on in our house that are strange, do you have…." She had almost told Barbra what was happening in her house when they heard a woman screaming loudly. "Help me! Help me!" They saw someone running down the street. It was Mrs. Bennett; she ran so fast that she tripped and fell over crying. "Help me!" She said, Sara grabbed Tessa standing to her feet to run over to her. Barbra ran over to her in her flip flops. "What's wrong sweetie! What's going on?" She yelled out. "My husband, my husband"! Mrs. Bennett said crying with her arms in the air. "Your husband, what happened?" Barbra asked her again. "He's not breathing, he's dead." She said putting her hands to her face. "He's dead!" Barbra and Sara helped her to her feet. "Come on honey, come sit down." Barbra told her. "I'm going to call the police sweetie; everything will be okay." She tells her as they walk back over to the porch sitting her down on the step. "Do you know for sure that he's dead?" Sara asked, just then Jonah came over to the porch. "What happened mom, Mr. Bennett is gone right?" He said looking up into the air walking over to the step near Mrs. Bennett. "Don't worry he will be okay." He told her putting his little hand on her shoulder. "Jonah don't do that go over there with your brother and play." Sara told him pointing out to William who was playing in the street with his friends. "Can I go inside to grab your phone?" Barbra asked Sara. "Sure, it's right on the table right when you open the door you should see it." She told her as she walked into the house. "How do you think this happened?" She asked Mrs. Bennett. "I don't know." She said. "He was fine, he had been working around the house all day doing chores he even did the yard." She tells her. "He never does the yard." She said sobbing loudly. "Hold on let me go inside and get you some tissue." Sara told her standing to her feet, holding Tessa to her hips. "Thank you." Mrs. Bennett said to her wiping her eyes with her hands. "How about some tea to calm you down as well?" She asked her. "No honey damn the tea, she needs something a little stronger than that don't you think?" Barbra said to her holding the phone to her face, waiting for the police to pick up. "Did you call a nonemergency line or something?" Sara asked her. "Yes, I did." Barbra told her. "No!" She said grabbing the phone. "You must call 911. She said dialing 911, handing her the phone back leaning over whispering to her. "What if there's a chance that he's still alive? He could be still alive over there," she tells Barbra. "No mommy he's dead over there, Shadow said so." Jonah said to them looking up at the stairwell. "Okay that's it you go sit down over there, don't move and don't talk, don't say a word!" Sara said to him in a stern voice. "Mommy don't get mad at me okay I'm just telling the truth," Little Jonah said to them going over to the couch to sit down. "You have to trust me when I tell you things."

"Jonah sit!" Sara tells him, handing a glass of water to Mrs. Bennett. "Thank you." She said taking the glass. "Sweetie after this is all over, I have a better drink for you over there." Barbra told her. "The ambulance and the police are on their way." She tells her, placing her cigarette onto her lip. "I'm going to go home Sara, let me know if you need help with anything later." Barbra said walking away slowly. "Barbra no, please stay I have the tea on and the kids are here playing, just until the police come please stay" Sara asked her. Barbra was reluctant she walked back over slowly. "Well honey if you want me to stick around, I have to light this cigarette, this is too much for me to handle without taking a hit of my cigarette." She tells her. "Oh, go on then light it up, just stand over there please." She told her pointing to the back end of the yard near the fence on the side of the house. "You know the baby won't get sick if I smoked close right, it's a myth." She tells her laughing. "Shh! Come one Barbra you know that's not true!" Sara said smiling at her as she walked away. They could hear the ambulance coming over. The sirens made Barbra's dogs howl. Mrs. Bennett stood up from the porch and walked over to her house to greet them. Sara waved over at Barbra. "Hurry up Barb come over when you're done smoking, I will be waiting inside for you." She yelled out to her. William and his friends played hide and seek all around the house, running up and down the stairs, all around the house. Going in the rooms and bathrooms hiding from one another, sometimes alone sometimes with one another. William ran with his two friends from school, Johnathan and Melissa. They hid in his parent's room under the bed they were being so quiet, they knew no one would come to look for them. They laughed taking turns peeking out to see if anyone would come for them. Melissa giggled and covered her mouth looking over at William while Johnathan peeked out. When Melissa turned to look over at Jonathan there was a face staring back at her, it was staring moving its head back and forth staring back at her then Jonathan. She screamed holding her hand to her mouth, closing her eyes, pushing with her knees for Jonathan to move out of her way so she could get out from under the bed. "Hey! Hey! What's wrong?" William yelled trying to grab her by her shirt. She jumped from her knees once she was out and ran to through the door screaming. Jonathan ran out behind her. William slid out from under the bed behind them trying to catch up with them. When he got out, he began to hear the beating of the drums. He stood to his feet catching himself from falling back down. He was afraid to move. He knew that those drums meant that the Indians were around somewhere. He looked around the room anxiously awaiting their presence. "Mom!" He yelled out. "Mom!" He began to run toward the door when it shut right in front of him. He was shoved to the ground, the drums sounded louder and louder as he scrambled around the floor to get away from whatever would come next. He was being pulled by his ankles to the closet, he tried to yell and scream but it was as if someone was covering his mouth. He couldn't speak, he fought kicking his legs away from whatever it was that was holding his ankles. His back was burning like fire, it pulled him so fast that the air hit his face. "What do you want?" He yelled out, just then the drums paused, he was shoved into the closet. It was dark, he was shaking so bad. The drums began to play loudly again.

The Way Back

William was in the closet screaming for help, no one heard him. Sara was feeding the baby and Jonah. The neighborhood kids ran out of the house screaming. Sara jumped up grabbing Tessa from her highchair, pulling Jonah by his shirt from his chair, tugging him to the front door to see where the kids were running to. She was looking for William, calling out for him as they screamed running down the street. She leaned from the doorway looking for him, calling out for him. "William! William!" She yelled out. She held onto Tessa and Jonah keeping them close to her. She shut the door going inside. What should she do? What were they yelling and screaming for and where was William? She thought, as she walked over to grab her cell phone to call Mitchell. It was so hard to reach him on the ship, the lines where always busy. She could hear the muffling of Williams voice coming from upstairs, she clutched Tessa to her waist side, pulling Jonah alongside her by his shirt. "I'm coming son!" She yelled out, "Hold on I'm coming!" She said running up the stairwell. Her feet hit the stairs; the sound of the wood creaked with every step she took toward the top of the stairs. When she reached the top, she called out to him "William!" She yelled again, "Where are you son?" She yelled. "I can't hear you baby help me find you!" She yelled out. "Help me find you!" She put Tessa and Jonah on the bed near the closet. She knew that William was inside the closet. She could hear his voice muffled, screaming for her help. She walked over to the closet door afraid it would be locked to where she couldn't get in to get William, but she had to do it, she had to open it to get him out. She cringed holding her breath, taking a dry swallow. She pulled the door open to find William hanging upside down from the light switch in the closet, his feet tied in knots, his wrist tied together. He was blind folded his mouth covered with a cloth that she'd never seen before.

"William what happened, how did you get tied up like this?" She asked grabbing at his arms to try and get him down. "I don't know how I am going to get you down from here." She said to him. "Did your friends do this?" She asked him. He shook his head no while she struggled to get him down. She kept her eyes on Tessa and Jonah. "Don't you guys move you hear me, don't move!" She yelled to them as she tried to get William down. "I have to get a knife to cut you down." She tells him trying to unravel the cloth from his hand and feet. "I will be right back." She tells him. "I have to leave you here William don't move." She tells him going over to Tessa grabbing her up from the bed, snatching Jonah by his shirt again. "Oh God help me!" She said as she ran with the children to get a knife to cut William down. "Hold on baby, mama's coming!" She said running to the get the knife. Jonah was being pulled around like a small doll, Sara was so stressed, but she knew she couldn't leave them alone at any time. She ran back up to the room placing Tessa on the bed, standing Jonah next to her. "Don't move Jonah, do not move." She told him giving him a stern look. "Okay I'm here son!" She said taking the knife to the cloth around Williams hands. "What happened, who hung you up here?" She asked him, cutting the ropes. "Was it your friends?" She asked him. William shook his head no. "It was the Indians mom." William told her. "What Indians?" The ones who want the hand drum back or the ones who took it?" "I don't know?" He said looking scared. "I have to find it mom can you help me find it?" He asked her. "There was a face looking at us under the bed, a very scary ghost face." He said in a panic walking around the room, pacing the floor in front of her. "I think I'm going to give Sabian's family a call again." She said, reaching into the front pocket of her sweatshirt grabbing her phone out to call. "Do you know if they would be home now son?" She asked. "You have to remember we are 3 hours behind them, it's already well past midnight there." He told her sitting on the bed next to Jonah, picking up the toy handing it to Tessa. Sara called the number; the phone just rang and rang. She left a message when the voice mail answered. "Hi this is Sara your old neighbor, I left a message earlier for you to call me back as soon as you can I believe that your son gave my son a gift before he left, it was a hand drum, if you can please call me back I'd appreciate it, call me any time thank you!" She said hanging the phone up. "Okay William where did you last have that drum?" She asked him. He stood up scratching his head. "Mom, I fell asleep with it in my hand the night we moved in, I shook it until I fell asleep. When I woke up it was gone!" He said looking around in the closet. "I thought maybe it was hidden in the sheets I slept on, but it wasn't there it was just gone." He said.

"I know where it is." Jonah said smiling. "Where baby?" Sara asked. "Shadow has it and he says he'll never give it back because if he does, we won't be able to play anymore." Jonah told them. "Where's shadow now?" Sara asked him. Jonah pointed to his room door. "He's in there all the time or just now?" She asked. "He stays there when

I'm not home." Jonah said smiling. "He has other people with him, two girls and boys, we play all the time together mom I like them all!" He tells her with excitement. "Jonah they aren't real people baby, they don't belong here." Sara told him grabbing his by the hand. "You guys come on grab your things, I need to go somewhere to think." She said picking Tessa up from the bed clutching her to her hip while grabbing Jonah's hand again. She took them down the hall, passing Jonah's room slowly almost tiptoeing away from the rooms heading downstairs. "Do you see any of them out here Jonah?" She asked. "What do you mean mommy, they're everywhere we go, they're not going to leave us alone with the Indians. Shadow told me that they are dangerous." Jonah went on talking as they walked down the stairs. "Hmm, why would the Indians be dangerous?" William asked him. "I don't know." He said shrugging his shoulders. "They just are." He said grabbing one of his toys from the floor when they got to the bottom of the stairwell. Sara went over to the living room area to grab her purse clutching Tessa to her hip, the doorbell rang.

Sara peeked out from the window; it was a very tall man. He waved hi, trying to get a look inside. "Can I help you?" Sara yelled out from the inside of the door. "Hi, I'm looking for William." He said. "William?" She responded, "Yes, is there a William living here?" The tall man asked. Sara looked at William shaking her head as if to tell him to be quiet. "Shh!" She whispered. "No there's no William here sorry sir." "Are you sure ma'am?" The man asked, reluctant to leave. "I know I have the right home ma'am; I've seen it all before." He said stepping away from the doorstep. "I can't help you if you don't let me in." He said as he began to walk away, he kept looking back at the house as if he thought Sara would open the door. He started humming. The humming was so loud that Sara could feel it in her chest. She held her hand to her chest and tears rolled from her eyes down her cheeks, she slid down to the floor clutching onto Tessa with her purse on her shoulders while the boys watched her. They grew sad to see their mother break down as she did. "Mommy don't worry." Jonah said, wrapping his little arms around her neck as she sat on the floor sobbing. "I just can't anymore." Sara said sobbing. "I can't run anymore, I'm tired, I don't know what to do anymore." She said with her head down low. The boys hugged her while she sobbed on the floor. Just then the phone rang. Sara wiped her eyes taking her phone from her pocket looking down to see who it was. The number was an unknown number, she answered it anyway, hoping it would be Sabien's mother or someone who would know how to reach them. She had recently reached out to the ombuds-man on base there to find them. "Hello." She said sniffling. "Hi, is this Sara Clark?" The woman said on the phone. "Yes, it is how can I help you." She asked, "Hi this is Amy I'm the base ombudsman, how are you?" "Hi, I'm doing okay, did you find out any information on the Musksogee family? It's very important that I find them." She told her sliding Tessa from her lap onto the floor.

"As a matter of fact, I called the family and they said they had been trying to reach you for months and they couldn't get through with any of the numbers they have for you, even the kids tried." She tells her. "What do you mean, do they have the right numbers?" Sara asked her. "I believe so." The woman tells her. "Here, let me read the numbers they used, she began to read the numbers off that they used to try and call them. "They are all correct." Sara told her. "I don't understand why they would be unable to reach us?" Sara said to the lady. "I've tried calling them as well but the phone just rings and I get the voicemail." She tells her. "Okay well I have an idea ma'am if you have the time?" The woman Amy says to her. "Sure, I have time." Sara tells her. "Well what I can do is use this phone feature that we have on base to connect you to them, is that something you'd want to do? It's three way calling, are you familiar with that?" She asked. "I am Amy." Sara said to her. "Okay well this is what I will do, I'm going to hang up with you and call Mrs. Musksogee to see if this is a good time to connect with her, is that okay?" She asked. "Yes, it is, I will be waiting." Sara told her hanging up the phone. She grabbed Tessa from the floor and picked up her purse. She walked over to the couch sitting down with the boys and Tessa. "Will they be able to help us mommy?" William asked. "I don't know son I hope so, look turn the tv on put on a movie for you and your brother." She tells him. "I will handle this." She said sitting Tessa next to William. "Mommy do you think if we go stay with grandma and grandpa these things would stop happening to us?" He asked. "I don't know son, I just know we have to find that hand drum and get it back to where it belongs, my gut tells me that it is the sole reason for this problem we're having." She tells him, standing up walking over to the stairwell. "William, I want you to do me a favor." She says. "I am going to go upstairs to look for the drum in your room. I want you to sit here and hold onto Tessa, don't move no matter what happens don't move. Jonah come here." She says holding out her hand to him. "Listen I want you to sit right here, don't move even if you hear something upstairs don't move okay baby." She tells him sitting him on the other side of William. "William don't let him out of your sight don't move, okay?" She said taking her hands to her pocket clutching her phone. "I will be right back you guys remember don't move." She said running up the stairs. She had to find the hand drum. When she got to the top of the stairs she stopped, staring down the hall at William's room first. She walked slowly down the hall to his room opening the door slowly going inside. She blew her hair from her face. "Here go's nothing." She said softly going to his closet, looking through the clothes, feeling on the shelf. She was on her tippy toes trying to reach all the way back to feel for it. She pictured it being a medium size drum that had a stick to hold it in your hand, she knew it had to have colors on it.

Her search in the closet turned up nothing. She kept looking around on the bottom of the closet, she found nothing under the bed either. She began to grow very frustrated. she pulled everything from William's drawers, only making a mess. She even looked inside his shoes turning them upside down, shaking all his pants upside down, checking for anything that may resemble the drum. She went from William's room to Jonah's room, doing the same thing. She went into Tessa's room and stood in the middle of the room. "Wow this is really sad, my baby never got to enjoy his room." She said softly to herself. Suddenly she hears the drum, it was coming from Tessa's closet. She turned looking over at the closet door, it was cracked slightly. She walked slowly over to the sound of the drum taking a deep breath. She walks over to the door quickly opening it, standing before her was a very tall Native man. His bright red feathers flowing over the top of his head. His face covered in red and white paint. Startled she jumped back screaming loudly, slamming the closet door shut with her back leaned up against it to keep it shut. She covered her mouth. "This isn't real, this isn't real." She said to herself shaking her head. She took a deep breath she could still hear the drum beating inside the closet. She stood up straight staring at the door. "I must do this, I have to search for the drum, maybe the sound of it beating is a sign that it's in there." She thought as she stood back with her hand reaching out to open it again, her phone rang loudly, startling her. She jumped putting her hand to her mouth, muffling a scream. The light from her phone shined through the darkness, ringing over and over. She scrambled through her pocket grabbing the phone.

"Hello!" She said in a hurrying tone. "Hi this is Amy the ombudsman over here at Fort Drum in New York. "Hi, so did you get ahold of her?" Sara asked. "I did, she's on the line. "Hi! How are you?" Mrs. Musksogee said loudly. "How are you all doing?" She said to Sara. "We are okay, I have been trying to get ahold of you for a few weeks." Sara told her. "Yes Ms. Amy told me that, I was surprised because I have been trying to get ahold of you as well." She tells her. "Please can you tell me about this hand drum that was given to William from Sabien?" Sara asked. "The drum needs to be given back; it belongs to the reservation. It's a very important symbolic ritual piece that belongs to the elders of death on the reservation." She told Sara. "Elders of death, what does that mean?" Sara asked, "It's very important that you get it back to us so that we can take it back to the reservation, it's dangerous." She tells Sara. "Dangerous?" Sara asked. "Yes, Sabien has been forbidden to go on the reservation until the drum is returned, the drum is spiritual it can bring the spirits up to the flesh." She said. "Spirits that are not always nice." She said to her. "I need you to tell me what to do." Sara said. "Something has been happening to us since we've been here, something terrible.

There has been Indians and old pioneer people around us haunting our family." She tells her. The phone is quiet. "Hello Mrs. Musksogee! Hello!" Sara says. "Hello!" There was the sound of static coming from the line. She could hear Mrs. Musksogee talking in a faded voice in between the static. Suddenly the line went silent. "Hello Mrs. Clark, I think we lost her." The ombudsman said loudly. "I'm going to try and to try and get her back.

Heavy Rain

Sara tried to call Mrs. Musksogee to finish talking about the hand drum. She needed to know what to do immediately. The last words she heard from her was that the drum was dangerous. She continued looking around the house, skipping the closet in Tessa's room so that she wouldn't see the Indian man again. As she looked around the house, she could hear the beating of drums. She went into every room where she could hear it and searched around only to come up empty handed. She even went into the bathrooms; the two upstairs were dark and cold. When she went in, she searched the cabinets and all the drawers moving everything out of the way. There was nothing there. When she got to her bedroom, she hears William screaming for her to come. "Mom please come now!" He yelled out. "William what's wrong?" She yelled running from her room to the stairwell. She took off full speed when she felt a push on her back, two very big hands shoved her to the floor. She fell flat onto her face, turning over quickly onto her back to look up, it was the pioneer woman dressed in a blue dress with ruffles down the bottom and short black boots. Standing next to her was another woman dressed like the other, but her hair was pinned up into a bun with a little hair alongside her face. The one woman shook her head no, the other one put her finger to her lips. "I told you not to leave the baby alone!" The taller woman told her. She could hear William screaming for her. She kicked at the women, scooting her body across the floor to get away from the two of them.

They came after her rushing toward the stairwell behind her. One of them tried to grab hold of her feet, she kicked and scooted as fast as she could. "Mommy! Mommy!" William yelled. Sara made her way to the top of the stairs trying to stand to her feet. She was being shoved and tugged by the two-pioneer ladies. She struggled to fight her way away from them, pulling her sweatshirt from the grips of their hands. They grabbed at her, poking her and slapping at her as if they were trying to distract her from going down the stairwell. On her knees holding onto the wall, she grabbed on as tight as she could trying to stand to her feet again when the two women looked at one another and smiled. Sara jumped to her feet rushing to go down the stairwell holding on to the rail. She was shoved so hard that she fell sliding and flipping all the way down to the bottom of the stairs. She fell to the ground looking up at the children, then back to see where the women were on the stairwell. They both stood side by side smiling at her as she held her head. She looked back at the children. "William call daddy!" She said before passing out on the floor. Jonah and Tessa began to cry. William held onto Tessa running over to his mother to try and wake her. "Mommy! Mommy! Please wake up!" He said tugging at her chest "Mommy!" He screamed. Tessa and Jonah held onto his shirt looking out toward the window, the tall man was back staring in at them. This time there were two women with him. Their hair was braided down their backs. There skin was brown. They both wore a red feather tied into the braid on top of their heads. They knocked on the door. "William, we can help you if you let us in." The man said pointing at the doorknob.

William grabbed his mother's phone from her pocket. He dialed his dad's number quickly. "Go away!" He yelled out to the man and the women standing in the window. "Go away, I don't want your help!" He said as the phone rang waiting for his father to pick up. They looked at William, the man began to hum loudly, the women hummed the same tune. It was so loud they could feel the vibration of their voices throughout the walls of the house. "Hello dad!" William said loudly. "I need you to come home mommy fell from the stairs and there's a man at the door with these women they're trying to get into the house daddy please! Come help us!" He said sobbing to his father, watching as Jonah and Tessa covered, their ears so that they couldn't hear the humming. William sobbed so loud. "Okay son I'm on my way, stay on the phone with me okay, don't hang up!" He told him running through the crowd of people working on the ship. "Hey where are you going?" One of the officers asked him, rushing behind him. "You know we can't leave right now we're testing. "I don't care I have to go, something happened at home please let them know I had to go!" He said. He ran all the way to his car. "Son did you try waking your mother?" He asked William. "Dad she won't wake up, she's out, she fell really hard down the stairs." He tells him sobbing. "Okay take your siblings and go into my bedroom." "No dad, I don't want to leave mom." He tells him sobbing. "Okay, okay son, is she bleeding anywhere?" He asked. "Her head is bleeding, she's out." He tells his dad. "Okay son hang up with me dial 911 hurry!" He tells him hanging up the phone, rushing to his car, getting in.

When he began driving the rain fell heavily. It began to storm hard suddenly. Mitchell was so scared he was sure Sara was hurt. He had to drive slowly to make it home safe.

William dialed 911, telling the operator that his mother had fallen from the top of the stairs, and she wasn't speaking. "Mommy!" He said slapping her face gently, trying again to wake her while the 911 operator stayed on the line with him. "Someone will be there soon, what's your name young man?" The operator asked him. William was sniffling so hard; he was devastated at seeing his mother this way. "Don't cry son, are you the only child in the house?" She asked him. "No, I have a sister and a brother." He told her still sniffling, crying softly. "When your mom fell were you guys the only ones around?" She asked him. "No there was a man and two women at the window. I called for her to come to see who they were, and that's when she fell." He tells her. "Are they still at the window?" She asked. "William looked up not realizing that they had gone, that the humming had stopped, and they weren't there anymore. He paused for second looking all around the room. "No, they're gone." He tells her. "Were they inside the house or outside the house?" The woman asked. "They were outside the house." He tells her wiping his nose with the top of his shirt, still holding onto Tessa. "Okay son, they are driving up now and the ambulance is right behind them, tell them exactly what happened to your mother." She said, "Everything will be okay now William, open the door for them okay." She said, coaching him to open the door. "Thank you." William said walking over to the door with Tessa on his small hip. He opened the door slowly. "Hi, can we come in?" The officer asked, "Okay good luck." The operator said hanging up.

"Sure." He said pulling away from the doorway, making away for them to come in. "What happened?" The officer asked. "My mother fell from the stairs." William told him. there were two officers, one woman and a man. "I'm officer Terrel and this is my partner officer Janice." He tells him. "Can you tell how it happened?" He asked. "I don't know, she just came flying down the stairs." He told them looking up at the stairwell. "Is there anyone else here with you guys?" He asked. "No just mommy." He told them. "No there's my friend Shadow, he's been watching from the stairs." Jonah said pulling on the officer's pants leg. "No! no we're alone, just us and mommy." William assured them as the ambulance workers came inside, rushing to Sara laying lifeless on the ground. "He has an imaginary friend name shadow." He tells them smiling, still sniffling. "He likes to tell people that he's here but he's not here." He tells them while the EMT checks over Sarah. Mitchell runs into the house. "Are you all okay? He yelled, grabbing Tessa from William, standing over the EMT workers as they worked on waking Sara up. He began to sob. "Is she okay?" He asked. "Well, she's breathing, she hit her head pretty hard, we are going to take her to the hospital you are hubby, right?" Officer Janice asked Mitchell. "Yes I am." He responded. "Can you follow them to the hospital?" She asks. "Do you have anyone who could look after the children while you go, like a neighbor or a close friend we could call for you?" Mitchell shook his head no. "Thank you for your service by the way, if we weren't on duty, we'd babysit for you." The officer told him shrugging his shoulder.

"Is everything okay?" A loud country voice said from the doorway. "Hi, do you know her?" The officer asked. It was Barbra from next door. "Hi, is she okay?" She asked walking into the house while the EMTS placed Sara on the bed to go to the hospital. "She's bleeding, oh my! Is she okay?" Barbra asked again. "We don't know ma'am we are going to transport her to the hospital, she's hit her head pretty hard, she's unconscious right now." The officer explained. "Do you live over here close?" He asked her. "Yes, I live next door, how can I help Mitch?" She asked. "If you can keep an eye on the children while I go to the hospital with her, I'd really appreciate it." He tells her. "Sure, no worries I can do that Mitch, I will take them to my house, is that okay?" She asked. "Sure, it's fine, can I have your number to call and check on them while we're there?" Mitchell asked. "Sure you can." She recited her phone number to him while he put it in into his phone. He handed Tessa over to her. "Wait let me get you a few diapers." He tells her, going over to Sara's bag to grab the diapers for her. "I don't know if they've eaten dinner yet." He tells her. "Well, I haven't fed my troop yet so it's fine, I will feed them and wait for you to come back." She said grabbing the diapers, pulling little Jonah by the hand and shrugging her head, gesturing William to come along with them. "I can't tell you how much I appreciate this." Mitchell tells her. "No worries, go on, go see what's going on with Sara, please call me let me know what's happening." Barbra said to him while they walked out together to the ambulance.

Barbra took the kids inside, they were happy to see the dogs running around and since her cats had died, she had gotten two new small kittens to replace them. Barbra's kids acted shy they'd always act that way even on the school bus, but William and Jonah had a way with kids because they moved around a lot. They knew that all it took was some common love of toys and games, and they'd get anyone talking and playing. Barbra had two boys, Sam and Steven. "Hey, do you guys have any board games?" William asked. "Yeah, sure we do." Sam answered. "What kind of games do you like to play?" He asked. "I like monopoly." William told him. "But I always win so it gets boring." He tells him kicking his feet from the couch. "What about play station, do you have one?" Sam asked William. "I don't, we aren't allowed to play video games." William tells him. "Wow why not?" Steven asked them. "Mom says they screw you up in the head." He tells them. "Hmm, well our dad is the IT guy at his job, he plans to get out of the service and make us our own games he's a genius." He said pointing over at his dad's computer desk. "See all that stuff over there? our dad can do anything with a computer including hacking into other peoples." "Hey shh don't say that." His brother said cutting him off. "Wow well he must have a lot of time on his hands if he's planning to make computer games." William said. "No, he's going to design some video games just for us." Steven said to him standing to his feet holding one of the baby kittens. "Did you hear what happened to our other cats?" He asked William. "No, I didn't, what happened to them?" He asked. Sam leaned over to his ear close, whispering softly. "They were murdered." He said smiling. "Murdered, what do you mean?" William said quietly. "I mean someone came into our home and murdered them." He told him. "No that's not true, was there an investigation?" William asked. "I don't know, I just know that they were murdered right there on that table, laid to rest all five of them." Sam said laughing. "Someone came in and sliced their necks then placed them there in a circle, and put feathers on top of them, like maybe it was a big bird who did it." Sam said laughing. "Why are you laughing?" William asked, "I never liked those cats, she treated them better than she treated us, so I was glad to hear they died." He said smiling.

"Hey, let's go play upstairs, I have some cool toys up there, you like Pokémon?" Sam asked. William shook his head no. "Geese where are you guys from mars?" Steven asked. "You don't play video games, you don't know what Pokémon is, you guys must be really bored at home." He said walking to the stairwell. "I don't want to leave my sister and brother down here." William said looking over at Jonah and Tessa as they sat on the floor playing with the kittens. "Oh, they'll be fine, my mother's right there in the kitchen, they can't go anywhere come on, I want to show you something." Sam tells him. William looked at Tessa and Jonah on the floor. They were content playing with the kittens on the floor. "Okay, I will come." William said following them upstairs. They rushed up the stairs to Sam's room. When they got into the room, flashes of lightening lit the hallway. They were startled by it, laughing and yelling at every flash of light. Sam began to count the lighting flashes, then the thunder. After about 10 minutes the rain fell. It rained so hard that you couldn't even see out of the windows, it was so dark. "Are you afraid of the rain?" Sam asked William. "No, I'm not, where we lived before it was always stormy and it snowed too." William told them. "Snowed, yeah we lived in the snow before, our parents are from Kentucky." Sam tells him." We go back for the holidays all the time just to see family and to play in the snow." Steven told him throwing a ball over to William "So you know why we don't talk to you guys on the bus right" Sam asked, "Why? William questioned. "Well ever since you guys moved over here, really crazy things have been happening, everyone's talking about it." Sam says throwing the ball back and forth from William to Steven. Steven shook his head as if to tell Sam not to say a word to William about the talk." "What are they saying?" William asked. "Oh, you know the usual your family's probably cursed or something, there's been so much happening since you moved in." Sam said, "I know you've seen how people look at your family, your mothers always looking afraid, she's always leaving the house in a crazy hurry dude, like where is she going?" Sam asked. "That's not anyone's business." William responded frowning up at the thought of what Sam was telling him. "I think I will go back downstairs now," he told them, tossing the ball to Steven walking back to the hallway. "I need to check on my sister and brother anyway." He told them waving goodbye. "Oh man I didn't even show you why I brought you up here yet." Sam said to him watching him leave. "No thanks I already told you I don't play video games." William said quickly walking away from the door. "I guess you don't want to see my surprise than! He yelled out to William. William walked off shaking his head. He went back downstairs to the couch where he'd left Tessa and Jonah playing with the kittens. "Hey William, are you hungry?" Barbra asked him, grabbing Tessa from the floor taking her to the sink to wash her hands.

"I made chicken noddle soup and cheese bread, is that something you'd like? I thought it would go along good with this weather." She said placing Tessa in the chair near her. "Come on Jonah here's some for you too." She said pointing at a bowel on the table for Jonah. "Boy's get down here it's time to eat!" She yelled. The boys came running down to the table fighting one another over where they'd sit. William shook his head at them. "Here one of you can have this seat." He said deciding he would just wait for his father to get back to eat. He walked back over to the couch scooping up the kitten from his seat holding him to his chest. "So, you're not hungry?" Barbra asked him. William shook his head. "No ma'am I will just wait for my father to get here, he's probably going to cook us something." He tells her snuggling with the cat. "Well don't say I didn't try feeding you." Barbra said to him opening the door to go outside to smoke. "Whoa it's still really raining out here." She said blinking her eyes at the sound of the rain. "I'm just going to leave this door cracked so that I can keep an eye on you all." She said putting her cigarette to her lips. "I'm watching you guys." She said smiling and moving her hand back and forth with her cigarette in between her two fingers. William grew more worried watching the clock thinking about his mother laying lifeless on the floor like that, he started to feel sad. Why couldn't he help her? He thought watching Barbra take puff after puff of her cigarette, the smoke filled the porch area along with the sound of rain. It was a bit scary to watch. William sat watching her until the phone rang. Barbra quickly put her cigarette out running inside to get the phone.

"Hello!" She said frantic. "Yes, is everything okay with her?" She asked she went on to listen to the person on the other end of the phone. When she was done, she hung up. "Okay boys your dad says they will be keeping your mother overnight just to watch her." She tells them. "But she's okay now, she has a bump on her head, but she'll live." She tells William and Jonah as she took Tessa from her sea.t "So is he coming to pick us up? William asked her. "Oh yeah he's coming, he'll be here soon." She said wiping Tessa's small face. "So, I guess you are a bit sleepy after all that soup huh baby girl?" She said holding Tessa up to get a good look at her face. "You are a beautiful little one!" She sat down on the couch and held Tessa on her lap rocking her back and forth. She started to hum the same tune that the man and the two women were humming earlier. It quickly caught William's attention, he stood next to her staring at her. "Is everything okay?" She asked him. William didn't say a word he just stared at her. Barbra went on humming. "Mrs. Barbra where did you hear that song?" He asked. "What now hun'?" She asked. "That song, where did you hear it?" He asked again. "Oh sweetheart, I don't know, it was just in my head I guess." She placed Tessa on a blanket laying on the floor near the window. The rain hit the window so hard. "She'll rest really good right there, the rain will keep her sleeping," she said walking toward the door humming the song the man and two women were humming earlier at the window. she put a cigarette to her lips and opened the door. "Okay guys I'm going to be sitting right outside here smoking don't go anywhere." She said closing the door.

"Hey, do you want to see my surprise now?" Sam stood up from the table asking William. "No thank you I will pass." He said sitting next to Tessa on the floor. "Well why not, I promise you won't be disappointed." Sam said looking upward and smiling. "I don't think you want to miss out William." He said. "I said no thank you, Sam." He told him clutching Tessa's blanket. "I'm good right here." He said watching the kitten fight with Tessa's blanket. Sam walked in front of him. "What's wrong with you? What's wrong with your weird family?" Sam and Steven started to taunt William, saying mean things to him over and over. "William the weirdo! William the weirdo!" William just turned looking out of the window watching as the rain fell. He wished his father would come in a hurry. Mrs. Barbra came up behind both the boys slapping them in the back of their heads. "Hey, stop it, I've already warned you both once about that, go to your room!" She said to them pointing up at the stairwell. William smiled at them giving them a wave. "Good night boys." He said to them. Jonah looked at them, he was holding a one of the kittens in his hand. "Yeah, goodnight you two meanies, maybe next time you'll be nice to us." He said tossing the kitten at them "Hey Jonah!" Barbra jumped to her feet from the couch. "Hey! Hey! Don't you ever do a thing like that again, you cannot throw animals at people, you got that!" She said taking the kitten up from the floor looking it over. "I really hope you didn't hurt him." She said in a stern voice. "I want my father!" Jonah yelled out. "You people are very mean people!" He shouted. William got up from the floor to grab Jonah, he was sobbing. "Come on Jonah just sit down next to us dad will be here soon," He said sitting down with him on the floor, he put his arm around Jonah "We'll be okay I promise." He told him. "I'm sorry about the kitten Mrs. Barbra he didn't mean it." He says to her looking her in her eyes. "Please forgive him." He told her.

Barbra rolled her eyes at Jonah. "My, My." She said to the kitten clutching it in her arms to her chest, kissing the kittens head. "Oh, he'll be just fine I'm sure of it." She said to the kitten rocking it back and forth. "Boys I must have another smoke. I'm taking the kitten with me." She said walking toward the door. As she walked out Mitchell was walking up the steps to her door. "Oh, hey you!" She said shocked to see him there. "I was just stepping out to have a smoke." She tells him holding the kitten in one hand and her cigarette in her other hand, between her fingers. "They're inside, the baby is sleeping." She said to him sitting down in her chair by the door. "The kids are ready to go." She tells him. "Were they any trouble?" Mitchell asked, "Oh no trouble just kids." She told him waving her hand up as if to shoo him inside. "Hey guys!" He said loudly. "You ready to go home"? He asked them. Jonah ran up to Mitchell hugging his waist. "Dad where's mommy?" Jonah asked. Mitchell walked over to the floor where Tessa was, picking her up in the blanket. "Mommy has to stay overnight at the hospital, we'll pick her up in the morning." He told them as they begin to walk toward the door. "Do you guys have all your things?" He asked. "We're not coming back for anything, so don't leave anything, make sure now." He tells them going through the doorway. "No dad, we have what we came with." William said to him pushing Jonah out. "Thank you so much for everything Barbra, if you ever need anything please don't hesitate to call me." He tells her. "No problem they were really good, anytime Mitchell, anytime." She said waving her hand goodbye. "Have a good night, Barbra!" He yelled out as they walked across the lawn to get home.

Found It

Mitchell took the kids home that evening, he was still so upset having to leave Sara in the hospital alone. He was even more upset about what was going on. He had no control, he felt hopeless. No control in his home, there was nothing he could do about the activity going on in his home, not even moving would help them. He made the boys go to their rooms tonight, knowing that Sara would have them sleep in the room with him. He was hopeless, uncaring, he couldn't do it tonight, whatever those spirits have for me tonight I will take it. He thought as he laid Tessa on the couch. He went over to the kitchen and grabbed a beer from the refrigerator. He sat down next to Tessa drinking the beer, shaking his head in disbelief of what they were all going through. I just don't get it, He thought, chugging back the beer. Why us and why now? He got up finishing the beer off, going back to the refrigerator to grab another, he also grabbed his bag from the couch sitting back down next to Tessa. He chugged back the beer and opened his bag taking his computer out. He began to search Indian hand drums and what it all means. He was able to find so many ritual Indian drum meanings, his head was spinning. He drank while he searched, he was very intrigued by all the meanings he'd found on the Native Americans. The hand drum he was searching for didn't come up quickly, although he hadn't seen it, he went on the description that William had given him. He searched the tribes in Canada and in Upstate New York where they were. He knew that Muskogee family was from the tribe that was on the reservation where they lived. He searched and searched drinking beer all night until he fell off to sleep with his computer on his lap, holding his beer in his hand on the arm of the couch he passed out there searching.

The house was quiet. Mitchell begins to snore a little, still holding his beer in a deep sleep when he was slapped across the chest so hard that the beer fell to the floor. His computer fell right on top of it, he quickly got up shaking his head, holding his chest, startled as anyone would have been being hit in the chest so hard. He looked all around the room to see if anyone was there, a little woozy from the beer he began to pick the computer up checking it out to make sure there was no beer on it. He sat it on top of the coffee table, then went to the bathroom and grabbed a couple of towels to wipe the beer up from the carpet. He scrubbed the floor with the towel going all the way under the couch to make sure he gets it all up. He reached way behind the couch and onto the side, when he began to feel something stringy, he grabbed and rolled it into the towel thinking it was just a doll with stringy hair, or some toy the kids lost. He sat the towel on the table, then went to grab a couple of paper towels to go over the floor one more time to get the smell out. On the floor he noticed there was wood sticking out from the towel, he dropped the paper towels on the floor near the coffee table and picked up the towel opening it up all the way to see what it was. He went over to the light to turn it up brighter to see, it was the hand drum! It wasn't damaged from the beer or anything. He was so excited he jumped up and down gripping it with his hand, he grabbed Tessa. "Come on baby girl!" He said excited. "I have to get this thing up to William!" He went running to the stairwell clutching Tessa on his hip, holding the hand drum in his hand. He started to yell for William. "William! William! I found it get up son!" He said busting into his room. "Hey son!" He said turning on his light. "Is this it? Is this the drum!" He said kneeling down over William getting into his face. "William is this it?" He asked again. William looked up at his dad with his eyes squinting shaking his head. "Dad what is it?" He asked. Mitchell had the drum right in his face. "Son this is it? Right?" He asked again. "Yes! Yes! Dad that's it!" He said sitting up rubbing his eyes. "You found it dad!" He said with excitement in his voice. "I did, I wish your mom was here we could tell her we found it son!" He stood up from the floor holding Tessa. "I'm going to keep it with me, we can't lose it again son." He tells him walking to the door. "Get some sleep son see you in the morning." He walked down the hall to his bedroom placing Tessa into a small playpen next to the window. He went into the bathroom to wash his face. He put the hand drum inside the belt strap on his pants so that he wouldn't lose it or misplace it. When he was done in the bathroom, he took Tessa back downstairs with him to get his computer. When he approached his computer, he noticed the search was brought up on the hand drum, it showed various hand drums and what they all meant to the tribal Indians. He couldn't wait to get up to his room to compare the drum to the ones in the search.

He quickly went up to his room grabbing Tessa crackers from the cabinet, filling her sippy cup with juice for her midnight snack. He held her close to his chest as he grabbed everything he needed. "Okay sweetie back to bed we go." He told her kissing her cheek. "Hold on tight to daddy's neck." He said as he walked quickly up to his room. He walked inside, sat his things down on the dresser, then quickly placed her into the little playpen next to the window. He moved the hand drum around in the waist band of his pants securing it so that it wouldn't fall out. He sat down near the bed in the chair next to the play pen staring over at the computer. "I am beat." He said in a whisper, but he knew that he had to figure this out for the sake of the family. There must be a solution before Sara comes home, he thought, getting up from the chair. He gave Tessa her cup and a few crackers. "Here you go sweetie, daddy has work to do." He tells her. He walked over to the computer picking it up from the table. He sat down on the floor next to the playpen where he could watch Tessa eat while he scrolled through all the hand drum symbols. Nothing came up looking quite like the one he held in the waist band of his pants, he took it out to compare it over and over. Reading the history of the Native Americans was quite the experience. Mitchell was intrigued at all he learned and although he was educated in high school history class nothing compared to all the facts on the internet about the Native American tribal history, he scrolled through so many stories. There was one, the Mississippi Caddoan Culture. This culture covered the Mississippi River all the way through the Valley to meet the Tennessee River, the Native American culture spread all around in the area.

Mitchell read and read until he fell off to sleep, this time with the computer on top of his chest. He dreamt he was being chased all around the house from one dark room to the next. He ran from the sound of drums and rattle snakes shook their tails all around him, he was running so fast and sweating profusely trying to hide from something he couldn't see. He was fighting so hard to get away from the snakes and the sound of the drums that the computer fell from his stomach. He tossed and turned trying to wake up still on his back. He begins to feel hands rubbing all over his chest and waist, he started to grab at the hand. A huge hand grabbed him by his wrist, as he began to open his eyes there was a very tall Indian man and three women in the room. The man was touching all over his belly feeling for the drum. Mitchell started to fight, pulling his wrist away from the man's grip. This Native American man hands were as big as Mitchell's head. The man started speaking to Mitchell in a different language. The women stared down at him speaking along with the man. Mitchell fought holding on to the hand drum as tight as he could without losing it to the Indian man. Mitchell tried to sit up, but the man held him down with his other hand. He kicked and squirmed around the floor trying not to wake Tessa. He held onto the drum until the women began moving away from the playpen as if someone else was coming in the room. Suddenly the pioneer woman appeared, she smiled down at Mitchell with her hair pinned tightly in somewhat of a perfect bun. She winked at Mitchell leaning down into the playpen.

"I will be taking her now." She said grabbing Tessa from her playpen. Tessa woke up and began to cry. "No! No! No!" Mitchell said, trying to escape from the heavy grip of the Indian man. "Let me go! Put her down now!" Mitchell yelled out. "Right now!" He said holding the drum in his hand, looking eye to eye at the Indian man as he held on to Mitchell's wrist as tight as he could, making them bleed. It felt as if his skin was being ripped apart. Mitchell held onto the drum refusing to hand it over to the Indian man. "Put her down now!" Mitchell yelled out as he wrestled his way around the Indian man. "I mean it lady, put my daughter down!" He said yelling loudly as the

Indian man grabbed him by his pants, picked him up
throwing him across the room away from Tessa. The other
3 women all begin to walk toward him. Then surrounded
the pioneer women holding Tessa. The man began to speak
in another language, the women were watching as Mitchell
fought the Indian man as best as he could. Mitchell was
growing tired holding on to the hand drum as tight as he
could, trying to keep the pioneer woman from walking
toward the door with Tessa. He scattered around the room
all around the Indian man as he chased him, holding onto
his clothing, tugging at his arms as Mitchell held the drum
above his head from time to time, he got out of the man's
way running as fast as he could toward the pioneer woman
he grabbed Tessa by her shirt, pulling her away from the
woman. She stared at Mitchell in a way as if to warn him
that he may be in danger if he didn't give Tessa back to her.
"Leave us alone!" Mitchell yelled, clutching Tessa and the
hand drum to his chest. "Leave us the hell alone!" He held
the drum up over his head and begin to shake it back and
forth. He didn't know what made him do it, he wanted to
taunt them with it, scare them to make them go away, so he
shook it. He kept shaking it. The strings hit the small drum
making a sound that would echo the room over and over.
The three women began to fade away, the Indian man stood
by the door staring at him, he soon faded along with them.

Mitchell had his eyes on them the whole time he's
clutching Tessa, tears flowing from his eyes, his wrist
bleeding from the Indians grip. The blood ran down his arm
onto his shirt he kept on shaking the drum as hard as he
could until he didn't feel they were there anymore. He cried
out, "What the hell is happening to us!" He held onto
Tessa's small body sliding down to the floor, still trying to
shake the drum, he sobbed loudly. Tessa cried with him,

William and Jonah came running into the room. "Daddy
what's wrong! What happened?" William asked him.
"Shadow came to help you daddy! he did I saw him!"
Jonah said looking down the hall. "As long as you shake
the drum they can't hurt us daddy, that drum will protect
us." He said. "Son who told you that?" Mitchell asked
Jonah. "He did!" Jonah said pointing down the hall.
"Shadow told me they need the drum to stay around, if we
return it or they get it from us they can stay here with us in
present time." He told his dad looking frazzled. Mitchell
got up from the floor wiping his eyes with the back of his
arm, still holding the drum, clutching Tessa to his chest.
"Okay boys grab a jacket we're going to stay with mommy
at the hospital tonight." He said to them. "But daddy we
don't have to run, you have the drum now they can't get us,
they can't hurt us, let's just stay put in the bedroom." Jonah
said to him. "No Jonah!" William said. "Dad's right, we
should just go to the hospital to be safe." William said.
"We are safe here." Jonah told them. Jonah stepped back
looking all around the room nodding his head as if he was
talking to someone standing around him. He stared down
the hallway. "Dad it's okay you should give me the drum; I
will give it them and we will be fine." He said, stretching
his little arm out reaching for the drum.

"No Jonah! Dad told him in a stern voice "We can't give
it to them, they can't leave if they get a hold of it, they will
stay they will be stuck here with us." His dad told him.
Jonah stepped back into the hallway looking behind him
"Daddy we can do this the easy way, or we can do it the
hard way it's up to you." He said, staring up at the walls of
the hallway shaking his head. "It's going to be okay daddy
I promise just give it back to them." He said to his dad.
"Jonah I will not, now grab your jacket let's go! Come on

William grab your sisters bag we're out of here now!" He said walking toward Jonah to grab him by the arm. Jonah stepped back further away from Mitchell as he reached for him, he kept moving away from him stepping back further into the hallway. "Jonah seriously, I don't have time we are leaving now come with us or stay here alone!" He told him standing still by the stairwell, waiting for Jonah to come along. Jonah stood there, looking back and around him. "Dad, give up the drum!" He yelled to his father. "Do it now!" He yelled loudly with his arms to his side, clutching his fist. He stood further back away from Mitchell turning his back. "It would be easier if you'd just give it up dad!" I don't want them to hurt you, do it now!" He yelled. The hallway lights flickered on, and off. Mitchell held on to Tessa tighter with his hand held across William's chest, moving them back as if to protect them from whatever may come next. The hallway went dark Mitchell reached around touching over William's face. "Here son hold onto your sister, don't let her go." He said handing her over to him. The lights came on bright Jonah was no longer standing in front of Mitchell. William clutched onto Tessa holding her to his chest, shielding her from seeing what was in front of them.

There was four Indian men standing before Mitchell staring down at him bigger than life. They stood still at first, the house was still, and quiet Mitchell didn't move as the one standing closest to him reached to grab the hand drum from his waist. Mitchell grabbed onto his hand, holding it as tightly as he could moving it away from his pants. "No!" Mitchell yelled out struggling with the Indian man to keep the drum. The other Indian man grabbed a wooden pipe from his side it was really neatly designed with men riding horses on it. Mitchell was still struggling with the other Indian man. He started to move away, pulling the man by his hand away from the other Indians as they all began to reach for the drum in his pants. Soon the man with the wooden pipe begin to blow it. He blew it into Mitchell's face Mitchell begin to struggle slowly as if he was moving in slow motion. William stood there helpless watching as his father's attack became more aggressive. Mitchell didn't give into whatever it was that the Indian blew at him although he was struggling, he wouldn't allow the Indians to overtake him or get their hands on the drum. He tugged and pulled away from them, the room went from dark to light, then darkness. William had tears running from his eyes as he watched his father struggle through his fight with the Indians, they now had Mitchell pinned up against the wall holding him still as the taller Indian man blew the wooden pipe at him. Soon the lights came on. Mitchell was still holding the drum in his pants, with one hand to the Indian man standing in front him, holding him back, he heard small feet hitting the wooden floor underneath them, scratching the floor running toward him. William looked down at the floor. Mitchell stood, holding his ground with the Indian man tugging for the drum, looking down to see what was coming. A very black cloud of darkness stretched out over the wooden floor covering Mitchell's feet, from his toes to his head it covered him. Mitchell resisted, watching how horrified William was of what he was seeing. He resisted shaking his head as if to shake the bugs off him, to no avail he was unsuccessful.

William stood back crying, holding Tessa. He was terrified as he watched his father covered in bugs from his head to his toes. He held onto Tessa tight when he saw the Indian men moving in on his father to grab the drum. He ran up standing in front of him with his back to his dads' chest. He held onto Tessa; the Indian men became more aggressive, angry at the fact that William stood between them, stopping them from grabbing the drum from Mitchell's pants. They began to grab for Tessa. They tussled with William as he turned from side to side stopping them from grabbing ahold of Tessa. He moved so fast that Tessa's head shook with every move. When he saw that they would persist he turned all the way around facing his dad's stomach, holding Tessa to his chest with his head down in his father's chest he held his eyes closed tight in fear as he felt his father shaking, trying to keep himself from breaking. William covered his father's hand, both covering the drum. One of the Indian men snatched Tessa from the side out from William's arms. He screamed "No! No! No!" He grabbed the drum from his dads' pants waving it in front of the Indians, threating to throw it down and smash it to pieces, but as he waved it around, he could see the fear in the Indian men's eyes. They began to fade away, backing away from them. William looked up at the drum, it lit up as he shook it from side to side. The Indian men backed away. The bugs began to clear away, running back down his father's body, scattering across the wooden floors following the Indian men, fading back into the hallway. William shook the drum as hard as he could holding it up to them. The Indian man holding Tessa placed her on the ground by his feet and begin to walk backwards fading away with the others. The lights flickered on and off, soon they could see Jonah down the hallway. He was watching, holding onto his cowboy friend's hand. He watched as they all begin to fade away. When Mitchell was no longer covered by the bug's he grabbed Tessa from the floor, walked up to William, grabbed the drum and continued shaking it. "Come on son get the bag let's go!"

He yelled out to William. "Grab your brother by the hand, let's go!" He said holding Tessa walking toward the stairwell still shaking the drum. They ran down the stairwell, out of the house into the car to go the hospital to stay with mom.

Whispers and Smoke

Mitchell made it to the hospital just in time for Sara to wake up to see them all in the room beside her bed. Mitchell was still a little shaken up by what he'd been through at the house. He held onto Sara's hand kneeling down close to her, clutching Tessa onto his hip with the hand drum tucked inside the front of his pants. He whispered to Sara. "I have the drum we are safe now." He whispered with a single tear rolling from his eye. Sara begins to sob turning her head away from the children. She stared out at the window sobbing silently so that they couldn't see. Mitchell rubbed her stomach with his hand then stood up from the floor to take a seat with the children on the small couch across from the bed. Sara turned to the children wiping her eyes.

"So how have you all been?" She asked with a smile on her face. Jonah turned to his father shaking his head. "Daddy took something that doesn't belong to him, now we're all in trouble." He said looking at Mitchell. "No son I took something back that doesn't belong to any of us, now go hug your mother and let's not talk about that at all." He tells him pushing him toward the bed. "I wish you'd just be quiet sometimes." William said to him putting his foot out to trip him as he walked toward the bed. "No, it's okay Jonah." Sara reached out her hand to him. "I get it." She tells him, holding his little hand pulling him close to kiss his face.

"So how are you, how's your head feeling?" Mitchell asked her. "I feel a little better, my head is still a little sore." She said rubbing the side of her head. "Hmm I bet you will watch your step now at home, right?" Mitchell said to her giving her a wink. "Yes of course I will" She replied smiling "By the way, why are you all here so late?" She asked. "The kids wanted to see you." Mitchell explained, before William could speak out ahead of him. "Oh, everything is okay now, right?" She asked Mitchell. "Yes, it is, we just needed to see you babe that's all, don't worry we are going to all be right here until they let you go home tomorrow." "Mitchell what do you mean?" She said sitting up in the bed. "You know you can't stay here all night with the kids honey, there's nowhere for them to sleep." She said to him. "It's okay babe we'll sleep right here on this comfy little sofa." Mitchell said, laying Tessa on his chest, scooting closer to the side of the couch to make more room for the two boys. "Mitchell, I think we can just go home." Sara begins to take the covers off. She tried removing her IV. "I don't want you guys staying here overnight." She said pulling the tape back from her arm "No Sara it's okay, I promise we'll be okay right here, we can't go home just yet Sara." Mitchell said standing, placing Tessa down on the little sofa. He went over to Sara grabbing her hands away from her IV. "I can't take them home just yet, it's not safe to go there, not yet." He tells her holding both her arms. "I figured out how to keep them all away from us, the drum has its own power in it." He tells her in a whisper. "What do you mean?" Sara asked leaning back onto the pillow. Mitchell looked over at William. "He did it, he found a way to stop them from attacking us and sent them back."

He tells her. "What how! How does it work?" She said, looking at William. He stood up and walked over to her bed holding his arm up over his head, he began to move his hand from left to right. "I just shook the drum mommy, I shook it twisting it and they faded away, they were angry, but they went away." He tells her. "So, they're gone for good?" She asked looking at Mitchell ."I don't know if they're gone for good I just know they left for now and I have the drum" Mitchell tells her "I there's got to be more to it though, right Mitchell, that was a little too easy" She said rolling her eyes up "Yes that's why we stay here tonight, we can go home in the morning get a hold of the Muskogee family to find out how we get rid of it without us having to go through what we've been going through." Mitchell said to Sara. "I think that's a good Idea, I believe they are going to release me in the morning before noon, here you guys take these pillows I can sleep without them." She said handing Mitchell the pillows from behind her head. "See we'll work this out it should all be fine." Mitchell told her, grabbing Tessa from the couch sitting her on his lap. He placed the pillow behind his neck leaning into it to get comfortable. "We'll do it all tomorrow." Mitchell told her. "Come on son sit down." He said to William. The next day came so quickly. Mitchell got up from the small couch holding Tessa in his arms. He went over to the sink to wash his face. The nurse came into the room along with the doctor to give them an update of the status of Sara's discharge. Mitchell walked over to the edge of her bed.

"So, doc, she's leaving this morning, right?" He said clutching Tessa to his waist. "Oh yeah she's ready." The doctor said. "Good morning by the way, I see you all can't live without her." He said with a little laugh. "Oh yeah the kids and I just wanted to be close to her that's all." Mitchell explained. "Oh no you don't have to tell me, when my wife is sick everything stops, and the kids can't do without her." The doctor said, smiling looking Sara over checking her head and her eyes. "But she's ready to go the nurse will take the IV out and she will just need to rest when she gets home and remember if she seems dizzy or is vomiting or having difficulties remembering her name or anything please bring her back, she'll need to be evaluated a little more should any of these things should happen." He tells Mitchell shaking his hand, smiling at Tessa. "Little one you get to take mommy home aren't you happy?" He says, handing the nurse paperwork, walking out. "Take care Clark family." He said as he shut the door behind him. The nurse began removing the IV and helping Sara with her clothes and shoes. "Do you need a wheelchair?" She asked, "No I think I can walk out of here, I'm okay." Sara said smiling. "Thank you for everything." She tells her, putting on her shirt. "Oh, it was a pleasure I hope you feel better." The nurse said as she left the room. Sara stood up to go to the sink to wash face and brush her teeth. "Boys get up it's time to go." Mitchell said waking them. They got up and went over to Sara at the sink. "Mommy we're leaving." William asked, "Yes son let's get out of here." She said running her hand through William's hair. "I'm so glad you're okay mommy." William says with a smile.

The family left the hospital arriving at the house soon after, as the drive was a short one. Mitchell helped Sara out of the car. William and Jonah followed him out leaving

Tessa in her car seat. Mitchell opened the door to the house and went back to the car to get Tessa. She was still sleeping. When they entered the house Mitchell laid her on the couch near the window sitting down beside her. "I'm still very tired." He tells Sara as she sat across from him on the sofa facing the window. "Well, you did sleep on the couch, that couldn't have been comfortable, here lay down." She said walking over to him with a throw blanket placing it over his waist. "You just get some rest now; I will take care of the kids." She tells him, covering kissing his forehead. Sara took Tessa from the sofa to her room. Jonah and William followed her up to the room to put her down. "Mom, we will be okay now, right?" William asked. "Yes son, we will be." Sara said, walking into the room to put Tessa down, until she noticed a foul smell coming up to the room. There was a line of fruit melons leading all the way into her bedroom. Jonah and William stood back looking at the fruit. Sara stopped short in her walk to the room. She stood still holding Tessa over her shoulder. "Son go downstairs, turn around hurry go! You too Jonah, go now!" She said turning away from the room rushing back down the stairs. "Hurry! Hurry!" She rushed them down. "Shh! Don't wake your dad just sit down, we'll go up in a few." She tells them, "Daddy has to rest he's going to work in a few hours." She tells them looking up at the stairwell. "What was that mommy?" William asked beginning to cry. "It was just fruit; I don't know where it came from, but it wasn't anything else." She said. "Don't worry we will fix it." She placed Tessa down on the couch and walked over to Mitchell. She pulled the cover from his waist, she slowly placed her hand on his stomach, reaching into his pants in search of the hand drum. When she found it, she held it to her chest. She reached in her pocket for her cell phone to call Mrs. Muskogee to let her know she had it.

Just when she called, she heard whispering coming from the top of the stairs. She went over to the stairwell. "Listen to me." She said to the boys. "Stay down here! Don't move I need to make this call and I need you to watch your father and your sister, sit over there close to them, don't move!" She said walking over to the kitchen, out of their sight. She dialed the number to speak with Mrs. Muskogee. "Hello can you talk?" She said as Mrs. Muskogee answered the phone. "Yes okay, you, have it?" "Yes, I do, I just came home from the hospital, will someone be coming to get it soon?" She asked her. "I will be contacting the elders as soon as I hang up the phone, oh and please this is so important to you and your family, do not put it down if you have it, they want to stay, they will come for you, they won't be happy, and they will send more spirits to rattle your household. Put it in a safe place where they can't get it." She tells her in a panic. "Okay but will they come to get it?" She asked. "They will and they will have to do a ritual to send those spirits back, they don't go willingly, they are very stubborn once they're out, please be careful because they know now that you can send them back, stay close to your family and watch for the smoke and the whispers." She tells her. "Smoke? What smoke and I hear them whispering now." She says walking over to the edge of the stairwell. "Go to your husband and children, shake that drum if you have it in your hand. It will keep them away from you all but you must stay close together." She tells her. "I will call you to let you know when the elders are coming, I'm sure they'll be coming right out to help with this. Shaking it will keep them away, but it also sets them free allowing them to come up more and more so be careful." She tells her. "The smoke is the older spirits the whispers are the newer ones recently passing on, beware of the smoke, the older spirits aren't as friendly, they are far more powerful and experienced than the younger ones. I'm so sorry that you are dealing with this, remember please keep it close to you, I will call you soon." She said hanging up the phone. Sara walked over to Mitchell; she placed the drum right back into elastic part of his pants on his waist. She sat down next to him watching as he slept. The boys sat on the floor next to her feet. Sara grabbed the remote to the TV, turning on a cartoon to keep them busy until she figured out her next move, she could still hear the whispering from the stairwell. She wanted to go up, she wasn't afraid anymore she knew that she could ward them off with the drum even if more came, she knows now that they are more afraid of her than she is of them. She waited anxiously for Mrs. Muskogee call, tapping her feet on the floor watching the stairwell. Sara was so tired of all the fear she couldn't think of anything else but this situation with the hand drum. Her family had been suffering, living in fear. This had been an awful time for all of them, they couldn't even enjoy the space they'd recently occupied because of the spirits. She contemplated going up, tapping her feet. She waited for her boys to stop looking back at her even though Mrs. Muskogee told her to stay close to the family she had to go upstairs, the whispering was driving her mad.

She stepped over the boys, quietly walking over to the edge of the stairwell to listen for the whispers. What were they saying? She wondered. "Mommy no." Jonah said shaking his head. "No just stay down here please mommy there's going to be smoke, I'm afraid of the smoke." He said to her, getting up grabbing her by the leg. She rubbed his head. "It'll be okay baby I promise." "No mommy the smoke is dangerous, don't go up there!" He said holding onto her leg and thigh. "Okay baby I won't, sit down over there next to your brother, I will just stand here to make sure no one comes down." She told him pushing him away. Just as he went to sit next to William, there was a hard knock on the door. Sara went to the window to peek out. "Can I help you?" She asked, looking out to see who it was. "Hi!" It was the man and the two women that had come in the rain before, they were humming. "Mommy no it's them." Jonah yelled out looking up at Sara. "No thank you!" Sara said, stepping away from the window, going to the peephole to get a better look at them. The man was an old Indian man dressed in feathered necklaces. He had a long ponytail; he wore cowboy boots and jeans. His belt was decorated. The women wore ponchos draped with prints of all sorts of colors, they had feathers in their hair. "Go away!" Sara told them. "Go!" She said, standing looking out of the peephole. The man walked away from the porch looking at the house staring upstairs. The women began to follow behind him, humming that same song from the other day.

Sara wanted to wake Mitchell, but she just couldn't. He needed his rest. He had to work at 3am. She sat back on the couch next to him, laying her head on his stomach, watching the children as they watched TV, Tessa on the smaller sofa napping. Sara fell off to sleep. Soon after she nodded off, Jonah ran over to her shaking her arm. "Mommy! Mommy! Mommy! Wake up! Please!" He screamed. "Look!" He pointed up toward the stairwell, there was smoke at the tip of the wall, flowing upward around the ceiling of the house as if something was on fire. Sara stood to her feet, running over to grab Tessa. "William get over here!" She yelled. "Mitchell! Mitchell! Get up!" She yelled. "Get up!" The smoke covered the top of the room. Sara stood still holding Tessa close to her chest, the boys holding onto her waist. Jonah crying out with his eyes closed. "Mommy they're bad, they're bad!" Mitchell jumped up from his sleep wiping his face with his hand, standing close to Sara looking up at the smoke. "Sara what is it what's going on?" He yelled out to her. Sara stared up at the smoke. "Get the drum out and shake it!" She yelled out at him. "Shake it, Mitchell! Shake it!" She yelled. Mitchell scrambled around his pants grabbing onto the drum, holding it over his head. The smoke moved faster toward them, covering the ceiling of the house. Mitchell began to shake it. The smoked circulated around his wrist as if to slow it down. Mitchell shook it as hard as he could his arm began to turn red as the smoke went around it to make him stop shaking. Mitchell reached up with his other hand grabbing the drum, switching sides shaking it as hard as he could. The smoke circled around Mitchell, as he shook it, he was covered in smoke. It was as if he was gone in the smoke. Sara held onto the kids as tightly as she could, standing back watching. She took them away from the danger of the smoke.

When William noticed his father struggling to keep ahold of the drum, he ran from his mother jumping into the smoke, grabbing onto his father, snatching the drum from his hand, falling onto the couch. He held it high over his head with his eyes closed shut. He shook the drum as hard as he could hoping the smoke would clear away from his father and leave the room. When the smoke began clear Mitchell fell to the floor unconscious.

Spirit For Keeps

"Mitchell! Mitchell! Please Get up!" Sara yelled
kneeling down to Mitchell, holding Tessa. "I need you to
get up! "Mitchell!" She yelled and yelled. The boys stood
by William still holding the drum in his little hand. Jonah
staring down at his father hoping he'd just get up. It was if
the smoke sucked the life out of him. Jonah sobbed.
"Mommy let's go before the smoke comes back, they'll get
us mommy they will, just give it to them!" He yelled out.
"Mitchell do you hear me! Get up please!" Sara yelled out,
holding Tessa in her arms tight. She leaned into Mitchell
with tears streaming down her face. He rolled over
coughing. "I'm okay babe, I am, grab the drum take it from
William now!" He tells her, pointing at William. The
smoke lingered above their heads from the living room all
through the house. Smoke and whispers from unseen voices
surrounded the room. Jonah ran over to the front door
twisting the nob. "Daddy come on! Come let's get out of
here!" He yelled out, trying to escape the clouds of smoke
in the room. "No son come here it's okay come here, we'll
be okay I promise!" He tells him getting up from the floor

going over to him. "Sara lets go in the room upstairs."
Mitchell tells her grabbing Jonah away from the door. They
all gathered near the stairwell to go up. "Mitchell there was
old fruit covering the floor up there." She tells him as he
rushed them toward the stairs. "I don't care, let's get the
kids into our room where they'll be safe.

Sara walked upstairs slowly, reluctantly following the
instruction of her husband. She walked up holding on to
Tessa with Jonah hanging onto her leg as tight as he could.
"Mommy I'm scared." He says as they get closer to the top
of the stairwell. "Don't be Jonah, it's okay, I got you."
William told him grabbing onto his hand. When they made
it upstairs, there was the old, dried fruit lining the middle of
the wooden floor on a direct path to the master bedroom.
Mitchell jumped ahead of the family, walking quickly into
the room first to make sure that it was safe. He held onto
the drum with his hand in the front of his pants. When he
entered the room, the floor was covered in a pattern of
feathers surrounding the bed as if to warn them not to go
near the bed. "Wait!" Mitchell said loudly stopping them
with his hand, holding them off from coming into the room.
"Mitchell what is it!" Sara yelled out. "Just wait a second!"
Mitchell yelled, not sure of what to do next. Just as she
yielded to his command the phone rang, she grabbed it.
from her pocket it was Mrs. Muskogee "Hello! Are they
coming?" She asked her in a panic. "Yes, they are, is
everything okay?" She asked, the phone was rustling in her
hand. "Hello! Are you there?" Mrs. Muskogee asked. "Yes,
I'm here I need to ask you, there was a pattern of fruit on
the floor rotten fruit, can you tell me why?" She asked her
in a panic. "The pattern of the rotten fruit is an old ritual,
are there feathers anywhere near the fruit, does it lead to
feathers?" She asked her. Sara moved close to the master

bedroom door. "Mitchell are you okay!" She yelled out. "I have Mrs. Muskogee on the phone!" She yells out to him. "Baby ask her about the feathers, they're all over!" He yelled. "The fruit lead to feathers all over the floor of our bedroom." She tells her. "Okay tell him to stand away from them, does he have the drum in his hand?" She asked. "Yes, he does." Sara says to her. "Tell him to hold the drum over his head, shake it while moving the feathers out of the pattern, move them around if they are in a straight line or in a circle, move them, break the circle." She tells her. "Mitchell hold the drum up, shake it and move the feathers around away from the bed, shuffle them from their form." Sara tells him, yelling into the room clutching onto Tessa with one hand, holding the phone in the other hand. She watched as Mitchell shuffled around the room in a circle, moving the feathers around with his feet. "Will it be safe when it's done?" Sara asked her. "Yes, when you all get in the room push all the feathers up to the door while shaking the drum, line the door with them don't leave any of them out, any one of them could allow the spirit to come inside the room." She tells her. "Okay Mitchell she says we have to come in when it's all done, is it done?" She asked, "No hold on baby hold on almost." He says shuffling around the room. "You okay?" Mrs. Muskogee asked Sara. "I'm okay Sara said crying looking at her children. "I just want this to end." She said to her. "It will sweetie, I promise they are on their way out to you, they will gather more Indian elders from the reservation near you as the spirits have been let out on their ground." She tells her. "It's very important that you hold onto that drum until they arrive, please let me know when they arrive." She said to her. "I will I promise." Sara told her. "Okay come it baby!" Mitchell said to her grabbing onto Jonah. "You guys get on the bed!" He said to them shutting the door then lining the feathers.

Across the door perfectly straight shinning the light down from his phone to make sure they are all there. "Baby nothing comes on in here, you'll have to use your phone light to go anywhere in her so be careful." He tells Sara. "What about charging it?" She said to him. "It may not charge from any of these outlets now." He told her. "I'll try the bathroom outlet a little later but for now please just get on the bed." Mitchell was covered in sweat, covered all over. He looked as if he'd been working out in his shirt that he'd worn for two days. "Baby I'm going to change my clothes I have to put my uniform on, but I want to wash up a little, here take the drum tuck it into the front of your pants don't move around too much okay, I'll be right here." He said shining his light at the bathroom door and the closet. Sara shook her head yes. "Hurry okay." Sara said to him pulling Jonah close to her. "It's okay baby come here, please don't be scared." She kissed him on his forehead. "And you William," she said reaching out for him. "You've been so brave through all this, thank you for grabbing the drum to save daddy downstairs, I was so proud of you, what a brave young man, you've become." She tells him leaning into his face to kiss him on the cheek. William began to cry, "Mommy I'm so sorry I took that drum from Sabien I didn't know it was dangerous, I didn't know it would do this." "Oh of course you didn't know baby, I'm sure Sabien didn't know either, you guys are just kids you don't know the consequences until it's too late, but the good news is there's a solution." She told him holding his chin.

"Mommy I'm hungry, aren't you hungry Jonah?" William asked. "Oh of course you are hungry, you guys didn't eat all day." She said to him, "I will wait for daddy to finish up and we'll go to the kitchen to get you all something to eat." She told them leaning back to rest her head on the pillow, staring down at the feathers. This would be a tough day; the spirits were very upset at them for having that drum. She thought about all that happened that day when she got home, Mitchell stuck in that cloud of smoke not being able to free himself, just when she was thinking of it Mitchell came from the bathroom in only his underwear. "Sara honey, look at this." He says to her, turning all around rubbing his stomach. "Look baby look!" He said panicked, "What the!" Sara took his phone with the light, she shined it directly onto Mitchell's skin. "Oh no!" There was a sketching of colors circling his body, round and round from his stomach to his back. "Baby what is happening to us in here?" He said holding his shirt, angry at the scars on his body. "It will be over soon." She said to him rubbing on his scars. The colors were bright. He stood back staring at the mirror rubbing his stomach. "Baby look at this." He said to Sara with tears in his eyes. Mitchell walked away from the mirror over to the closet. He went to get his uniform ready. He began to put on his T-shirt, he put it over his head bending forward, then he grabbed his pants from the hanger bending over to put on his pants. He began to feel pain in his stomach. "Sara, help me!" He yelled out. "Help!" He was hunched over with is hands straight out from his waist "What is it honey what's wrong Sara said running into the closet "I can't move! He yelled my stomach Sara help me!" He yelled out, Sara it hurt.

Sara pulled his T-shirt up. Mitchell's stomach was stretched out to his elbows there was a hand reaching out from his stomach. He fell forward in pain, the hand stretched around his stomach. The colors began to pour down his skin as if to dye his body with the colors. Mitchell started to choke, coughing loudly with his arms still stretched out, he was now on his knees coughing. His eyes watered of the colors in the circle on his body. Sara held onto him sobbing and screaming. "Mitchell! Mitchell!" Baby come on what is this?" She yelled out screaming. Mitchell fell forward onto his side, staring up at Sara with the colors running from his face. "Go to the children." He mumbled to her, she shook her head no. "Go Sara I will be okay." He laid there helpless, he knew there was nothing he could do, whatever this was it would run its course and be done with him soon. Mitchell crawled his way over to the shelves on the wall. He pulled himself toward the wall, lifting himself into a seated position, sniffling and holding his stomach. "Go to the children Sara, don't leave them no matter what!" He tells her. "I will be fine go!" He tells her again. Sara walked away backward, still worried about Mitchell. She watched as he struggled to catch his breath. Jonah and William were watching from the bed. "Is he okay mommy, is daddy okay?" Jonah asked worried. Sara shook her head yes, holding the hand drum close to her stomach. "Daddy will be fine." She told them sitting on the bed grabbing Tessa. "You boys lay down I will take you all downstairs to get food in a few, okay?" She told them, wiping the tears from her face with the edge of her sweater. "Mommy It's okay, we can just wait until tomorrow." William said to her, looking over at Mitchell on the floor of the closet.

"No, I know that you all are very hungry, I will make you guys some good mac n cheese it'll be quick and easy." She told them. They waited a bit for Mitchell to collect himself, he came out of the closet holding his uniform in his hand. He sat down on the edge of the bed looking very sickly and weak. "Hey, are you okay daddy?" Jonah asked him. "I am son, no worries, okay?" He said laying sideways alongside the bed. Sara rubbed his back. "Honey you're okay right?" She said to him. Mitchell shook his head yes in silence. "Baby I can't allow you to go down there alone with the children, we all go together, or no one goes at all." Mitchell said to Sara. He reached out for her hand. Mitchell's hand was as cold as Ice. "Mitchell are you okay?" Sara asked him again. "I am now, let's go get the kids something to eat." He told her sitting up. "You have the drum, right?" He asked her, holding out his hand to her for the drum. "Yes, I do." She responded reaching into her pants for the drum to give it to him. "No!" Jonah screamed out, don't give it to him, don't do it mommy!" Jonah screamed just as Sara began to hand over the drum, Mitchell turned to her, standing up in front of her with his hands stretched out straight, his shirt ripped apart, the hand from his stomach stretched out to grab it from her hand. Jonah jumped in front of the hand grabbing the drum, tossing it to William. "Keep it William don't let them get it again!" He yelled out. Mitchell fell to the ground breathing heavily. "Sara go downstairs they're here." He told her in a whisper.

Sara grabbed Tessa from the bed. "Come on boys let's go, William give me the drum son!" She said reaching her hand out to him. He gave it to her as they walked toward the door, crossing over the feathers was so scary for them. They all held hands as they crossed over. When they got into the hallway, there was smoke covering the ceiling of the hall. Mitchell lay still on the floor of the room, watching them walk down the hall. "Sara shake the drum!

Shake it up high!" He yells out to her as they fade into the hallway surrounded by the smoke. Sara began to shake the drum over her head, holding it up as high as she could over the children as they walked to the stairwell. The smoke began to fade away, but the sound of whispers began to get louder and louder, it was as if they were trying to talk to them, but the words were in a different language. "Sara help me up!" Mitchell yelled out, reaching for her hand to get up from the floor. "William, help me up!" He yelled out. Sara looked down at him holding the drum up over her head and Tessa to her hip, she was so afraid to let go of the drum in fear of the smoke coming back filling the room. William looked at his dad helpless and afraid. He thought if he helped, he'd be in trouble with the spirits in the room, he could hear them, he could see some of the shadows around him. Mitchell looked around the room. "Wait! Where's Jonah?" He yelled. "Where is he Sara?" Sara began franticly looking around the room. "Jonah come out here right now!" She yelled; they both begin looking around the room. Mitchell struggled up from the floor holding his stomach, they looked all around in fear watching out for the children while the whispers faded in and out of the room. William stood still, watching until there was a light near the window "Mommy!" He yelled out pointing his fingers. He pointed up at the light. "There!" He said as Mitchell and Sara turned to the light. There was Jonah standing with the shadows in the light. Sara stood back and began to cry, walking backwards back toward the stairwell. She was to upset, she clutched onto Tessa, holding her closer bringing the hand drum to her waist. Mitchell ran over to her as quickly as he could. "Sara don't put it down!" He yelled out to her hold it up high." He yelled. "I can't do this Mitchell!" I can't we need to go!" She yelled out. "Mitchell let's go!" She said falling over, holding the hand drum down to the floor. "I just can't do this anymore Mitchell I want to go." She began to sob. Mitchell ran over to her quickly taking the drum from her hand holding it up over his head.

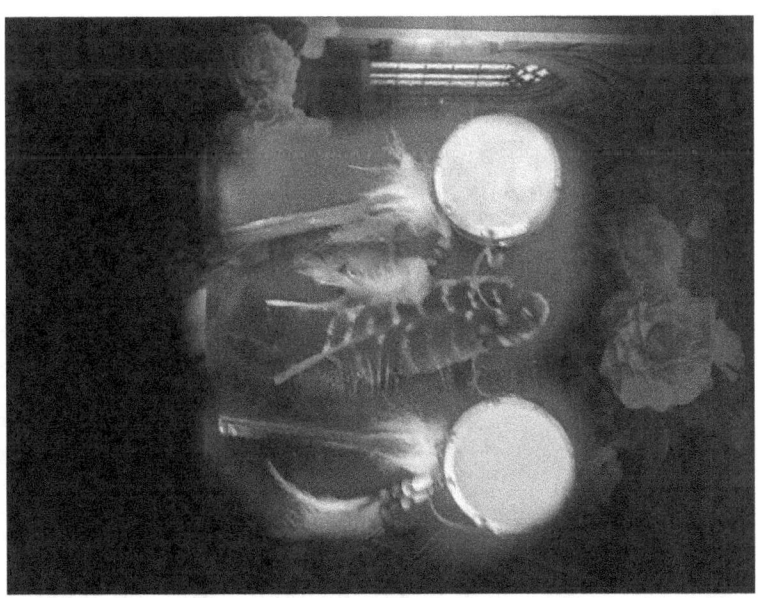

Tribal Fire

Mitchell held the hand drum over his head, he walked over to the center of the room standing face to face with the spirits. They surrounded Jonah holding him still with their hands on his shoulders. The older Indian man whispered into Jonah's ear as Mitchell turned the drum up and began moving it slowly side to side. Jonah shook his head at Mitchell. "Daddy, give them the drum and they will let me go!" He said loudly. Mitchell shook his head no. "William tell daddy to give it to them." Jonah looked out at his mother. "Mommy tell him to give it back now!" Jonah yelled out. "Mommy tell him!" He cried out. Sara walked over to Mitchell holding his arm down. "Mitchell, give it back to them, you can't keep it now, they have Jonah." She tells him. "No Sara it's a trick they can't keep him." He tells her. "Go over there stay by the door!" Mitchell yelled out to her. "Just stay right there!" He said as he went in closer to Jonah. Reaching out his hand to him, he called out for him. "Jonah come to daddy right now son, get over here." He said in his stern voice. Jonah looked up at the Indian men holding onto his shoulders. He looked back at Mitchell, shaking his head. Jonah was as quiet as he'd ever been. He turned away from the Indian man looking at Mitchell. "Daddy if you want me to come to you, you have to give up that drum, that's all they want from us and they will go." He told Mitchell as he stood there in front of them with his hand to the drum as tightly as he could. "I can't do that son you come over here now, we are leaving." He tells Jonah shouting at him in his stern voice. "Daddy I cannot." He told Mitchell. "They will not allow me to go, they will hurt us." Jonah says beginning to sob.

Sara stood by watching him sobbing, holding Tessa in her arms "Mitchell you have to give it to them I don't care anymore what they do with it, they can't have Jonah." She tells him. "I won't Sara it doesn't belong to them! Now we can get rid of them forever by giving it to the people it belongs to, or we can give it to them now and they continue to haunt us, they continue to scare us forever, no Sara, I won't allow it!" He tells her walking over to her. "Listen take William and Tessa, put them in the car we will leave soon." He tells her, beginning to push her toward the door. "Go on, he tells her holding the drum up over his head with one hand, shoving her back with the other. "You go wait with them in the car, I will get Jonah and bring him out in a sec, I promise." "No Mitchell he's not going to come they won't allow it without you giving up that drum." She said sobbing. "Sara trust me I will get Jonah go please, go to the car." He tells her, pushing her out toward the door. "Trust me." He tells her kissing her forehead. "Mitchell no just give the drum to them please." "Sara please do this for me, just get into the car please." As Sara opened the door slowly walking out, she noticed there was so many moving trucks in front of everyone's houses. Everyone was moving away. She walked to get into the car, she placed Tessa into her car seat strapping her in. She came back up to Barbra greeting her, standing next to the car door. "Hey Sara, how's it going?" She asked holding her cigarette away from her face going in to hug Sara. "I'm okay I guess." Sara said sniffling, looking all around the neighborhood. "You look a mess sweetie really; you don't have to lie to me." She said with a smile. "I get it, do you see this" she says taking a puff from her cigarette "Yep everyone's getting out of here, they say too many things have happened in their houses, scary things, if you know what I mean." She said. "No one really wants to be called crazy around here, so they are just asking to be relocated, when housing refuses them, they're all opting to move out in town, hmm I guess any place is better than this one, huh sweetie?" She said puffing at her cigarette. "For us we are going to Maine in a few weeks. I guess will hang on until then." She tells her walking toward the mailboxes. "Hey William." She said throwing her hand up waving her cigarette out at him. "Hi Mrs. Barbra!" William responded before getting into the car. Barbra stood by the curb staring down the street. "You have a good son Sara, I can't keep mine in the house, they leave, and they don't come home until they have to sleep and even those day's it's hard to keep them home, they absolutely hate it here, every night one of them wake up sweating and shaking from something they say they saw in the night." She shook her head. "I really hate we got stationed here, what a crock, me thinking I'm coming to beautiful California escaping the country life, well it was really okay until you all moved in." She said looking up at Sara. "Where the hell did you all come from?" She asked throwing her cigarette into the street shaking her head walking back toward her porch. "I'm sorry Barbra I really am." Sara said going over to the car.

Mitchell was standing at the door watching, making sure that Sara got into the car with the children. He closed the blinds when he saw that they were safe. He turned to Jonah standing with the Indian men. "Jonah, now I am going to shake this drum, you will move away from them as soon as I begin to shake it, do you hear me son." He said to Jonah. Jonah turned his head away from Mitchell. "Daddy go away please!" Jonah said. "I don't' want them to hurt you daddy, please go away." "They can't hurt me son, I promise they can't." He tells him beginning to shake the drum. "Daddy just go take mommy and William away I like them, they won't hurt me see Shadow over there, he won't let them hurt me." He tells Mitchell pointing at the stairs. There by the stairwell was the cowboy, he stood as tall as the door frame, his cowboy hat was brown, his jean jacket and jeans looked as if he'd been riding, his cowboy boots had spurs on them. Mitchell was startled that he could see the cowboy so clearly, he stared at him for a minute before the cowboy winked at him and tipped his hat. "Son come over here"! Mitchell yelled out to Jonah "Come over here now!" "No daddy just go!" Jonah says, running behind the Indian men to hide. Mitchell stuffed the drum into his pants, pushing the Indian men out of his way to get to Jonah. The Indian men stood still staring at Mitchell, stiff as boards they wouldn't budge to allow him to get to Jonah. "Jonah if you don't come to me son!" Mitchell yelled, "I will punish you!"

Mitchell reached around the men, pulling at Jonah, they blocked him, standing in the way of his hands. Just when he thought he caught ahold of Jonah's shirt, one of the Indian men grabbed him by his pants and shirt, holding him up as if he was weightless. He threw him to the ground, pointing at him frowning. Mitchell stood back up on his feet, twisted his pants around making sure the drum was safe, he felt around his pants, he ran back up to the men grabbing at Jonah. Mitchell was determined to get Jonah away from the Indian men. He was not afraid of what would happen to him any longer. He jumped into the middle of the men landing onto the floor behind him. The Indian men quickly grabbed Jonah turning him the other way standing, staring at Mitchell as he struggled to get up from the floor. When he got control of his footing Mitchell grabbed onto the table, pulling himself up to the wall. The Indian men watched him frowning, holding Jonah by the shoulder behind them. They covered him to where Mitchell couldn't see. Mitchell went running toward them screaming and growling as if he was a lion battling to get to his cub. He jumped toward them. They grabbed him by his arms, tugging him forward. Mitchell fought them as hard as he could. The taller Indian man grabbed Mitchell by the back of his neck squeezing it while bringing him down to the floor. Mitchell tussled around the floor with the man, he moved his body all around to get away from them. The Indian man gripped his neck tighter and tighter bringing him to his knees. They turned him over onto his back laying him flat while two of the Indian men held him down to the floor the taller Indian man began to grab at Mitchell's pants. Just as his hand went over Mitchell's stomach, there was a red light shining from it. Mitchell started to scream, he felt as if his stomach was being ripped apart. He bellowed out a scream so loud that it shook the room. "No!" Mitchell yelled out as the man tried to grab the hand drum from his pants. Mitchell shook his body around with the light shining through his stomach. He yelled and screamed, shaking himself away from the reach of the man. The man couldn't get to the drum. His stomach was hot to the touch. Mitchell struggled so hard to get away from them, he soon began to go silent. The room was dark, then red. It began to shake as if there was an earthquake. Mitchell lying still unable to free himself from the grips of the Indian men. He dropped to the floor as the room filled with smoke. The Indian men faded away. Mitchell was still on the floor watching as they faded, looking around for Jonah. Sara came running through the door.

"Mitchell! Mitchell! Are you okay!" She yelled, pulling Mitchell's head to her lap looking around the room. "Honey where's Jonah!" She yelled. "Where's Jonah?" Mitchell looked up at her shaking his head with tears running from his eyes. "I couldn't get him from them Sara, I couldn't get him!" He said sobbing on her lap. Sara held onto Mitchell. She pulled his shirt up from his stomach grabbing the hand drum, she threw it to the wall. "Here take it back please give us Jonah"! She cried out sobbing. They sobbed holding onto one another in defeat. Sara got up from the floor leaving Mitchell sobbing. "Jonah! Jonah!" She yelled running up the stairs. "Jonah! Come to mommy baby come out here!" She called out to him from the hallway near his room. She ran inside his room swinging the door open. "Jonah honey come to mommy please!" She yelled, "Please! Come to mommy son!" She fell to the floor in Jonah's room sobbing, Soon Mitchell was there to comfort her, holding onto her sobbing. The room door shut behind him. They soon began to hear the drums; the whispers were becoming clearer. "He stays, a voice says to them in a whisper. Mitchell helped Sara up from the floor, they opened the door. The sound of the drum was louder in the hallway and down the hall. At the edge of the room there looked to be a fire burning, in the fire was the shadow of Jonah, looking up at the cowboy holding his hand surrounded by the Indian men with red feathers flying from their heads. They walked around the fire chanting and beating hand drums. Mitchell grabbed onto Sara. "Baby let's go we can't do anything we have to get this drum back to the tribe; they won't ever let us have him this way." Mitchell tells her, running for the stairs to get the drum from downstairs where they'd left it. Mitchell scrambled around the room where Sara had thrown the drum, he put his arm under the couch struggling to reach it. When he grabbed it he got up and grabbed Sara by the arm. "Sara, come on we have to go!" Mitchell pulled her out the front door to the car. "What about Jonah, Mitchell, we just can't leave him here like this." She says. "Sara there's nothing we can do now come on!" He tells her getting into the car.

They Have to Go Back

They left the house racing toward the highway. Mitchell held his stomach tight with one hand and drove away with the other. William and Tessa sobbed with Sara for Jonah. "Jonah! Jonah!" Sara cried out as they drove away. "Sara, I promise you we will get him back, call Sabien's mother now, call her and don't stop calling until you get her! Tell her that they need to come here now, we lost Jonah!" He tells her trying to stay calm. Sara held her phone to her ear sobbing when Mrs. Muskogee answered. She didn't say a word at first, she was so upset she couldn't bring her mouth to utter the words that she had lost Jonah. "Hello!" Mrs. Muskogee said loudly. "Hello!" She said again. Mitchell took the phone from Sara, placing it on speaker. He dropped it in his lap. "Hello! Hello! Mrs. Muskogee this is Mitchell, William's father, we really need you to tell the tribe that they must get to California immediately they have taken our son Jonah, he's gone, we couldn't get to him." "You mean that the spirit has taken him to the other side with them?" She asked. "He is gone! Please tell them to hurry!" He tells her driving toward the Military base shipyard. "I am taking my family somewhere safe, but I need them to hurry and get here, please tell them that he's gone." "Okay I'm sorry! No worries, we will go to them now to let them know what's going on, I'm so sorry Mitchell." "Please let them know where we are. We want our son back tonight if we can get him back tonight, please tell them to hurry!" Mitchell said hanging up the phone, pulling into the gas station next to the Navy lodging area.

"Listen everyone please stop sobbing. "I promise we will get Jonah back." He tells them grabbing onto Sara's hand. "Lsten baby I promise you everything is going to be okay, they are going to come help us get Jonah and we can go back to being happy in our home, I'm going to check us into the lodge for tonight. I will go to the ship in the morning to let them know what's happening. We can search around here to see if there's anyone else who can help us, it's all going to be okay baby I promise." He said kissing Sara's hand with tears streaming from his face. Mitchell pulled into the Navy Lodge to go into the lobby. Sara sobbed along with William, "Mommy I'm so sorry I took that drum from him, I didn't know what it was mommy, I'm so sorry." He says sobbing about Jonah. Mitchell got a room with two beds, Sara got the kids settled in. She fed them whatever snacks were left in her purse until Mitchell brought them food from the commissary. She made sandwiches and gave them juice to drink. Tessa was still breast fed she'd eat a little, but Sara had to nurse her before she slept. After the kids were down for a little nap Mitchell waited, staring from the window for Mrs. Muskogee to call. Sara went over to him held him from behind. "Mitchell what are we going to do if we can't get him back?" She asked with tears in her eyes. Mitchell turned to her wiping her tears. "We will get him back; we have to get him back." Mitchell says pulling her close to his chest. "Are you charging your phone." "I am." Sara tells him, walking over to her phone to check for the call back from Mrs. Muskogee. "I hope they call us soon." Mitchell said sitting by the window holding his stomach. "I didn't think that I'd be back this time Sara." He said holding his stomach. "Let me see that." Sara said, sitting next to him pulling up his shirt, turning the light to his stomach to get a better look. "Geese Mitchell what the hell is this?" She said shaking her head. "It's almost like we are stuck in a dream." She said poking the rainbow of colors circling his stomach. "I don't know Sara this is the worst thing that could have ever happened to us, don't you think?" He said to her looking up with tears flowing from his face. "I mean what kind of man am I, I'm always leaving we are always traveling with the kids, for the good old Navy." He said putting his head down. "Wait Mitchell this has nothing to do with the Navy or you leaving, come on this is just a tragic mistake that happened between two kids who just wanted to keep their memory between one another alive, they had no Idea that this would happen." Sara told him, holding his stomach. "And honey, just FYI I love you, and the Navy has provided a very great life for our family, just look at us at the lodge." She said standing to her feet walking over to the kitchene.t "It's the most amazing place don't you think so?" She said, trying to make Mitchell smile. "Thank you, baby," Mitchell said walking over to Sara kissing her all over her face. "What would I do without you?" He said kissing her face, holding her close to him. "I promise everything will be okay."

Mitchell and Sara sat watching the kids sleeping on the
bed in the room. They sat close to the phone just in case the
tribe called for them to meet them back at the house. So
many families were moving out of the neighborhood. Some
of them not even acknowledging what they were seeing
around them. It was almost as if they'd just rather get away
so that they didn't see it anymore. Moving truck after
moving truck, that's all Sara thought about as she fell off to
sleep. They were all so tired, running was how they'd been
spending their time ever since they moved to California. It
was 3:25am when the phone rang over and over. Sara
missed the call twice before Mitchell jumped, startled from
his sleep to the ringing of the phone. William was staring at
him barely awake. "Dad, can you get that?" He said to
Mitchell laying back down onto the pillow. Mitchell
reached over Sara to grab the phone from the table next to
the couch. "Hello!" He said. "Hello, Mitchell it's me do
you have a pen?" It was Mrs. Muskogee. "Hold on."
Mitchell said grabbing the hotel pen and pad from the table.
"Yes, I hear you go on." He said shaking the pin for the ink
to come out. "Okay they will be at your house at midnight,
they will need you to remove everything from the living
room and the kitchen, they will also need access to dirt and
an open field of some sort, will that be a problem?" She
asked, "No it will be fine." Mitchell told her "Okay so be at
your house by midnight don't leave them waiting it's
considered disrespect." She tells him. "Okay, oh and before
I forget grab everything you can that you think Jonah
cherished in his innocence, that's the only thing you need
to have in the living room area." She tells him.

And the kids should be there as well, they will make a
safe space for them so don't worry, they will handle it all
from there." She said. "Again, we are so sorry our family

ask for forgiveness today and every day after." "No worries we know this wasn't the fault of your family." Mitchell told her hanging up the phone. "Sara, Sara, wake up baby they're coming!" Mitchell told her with excitement in his voice. "They called Mitch?" She asked stretching. "Yes!" He said waving the paper in her face. They will be here at midnight; they want us to come to the house." He tells her. "I'll just let the kids sleep a few hours longer." She tells him, straightening up the room throwing away the trash and food they ate earlier. "Is it going to be okay." She asked Mitchell. "I don't know, I'm a little scared but I know that they will help." When they arrived at the house Jonah was sitting on the stairs smiling with his toy car. He seemed to be waiting for them to come back when he saw the car pull into the driveway, he stood up to his feet and begin to wave at them. "Hi baby!" Sara yelled from the window. The car was still moving as she opened the door to race to him. "Jonah!" She said hopping out, running toward him. Just as she approached him, he began to fade away as if he were sand flying in the wind. The toy car dropped right in front of her feet. Sara began to sob loudly. "Jonah!" She yelled out holding her chest. "Baby come back!" She screamed. Mitchell went toward her to hold her. "It's okay baby, it's all right." He told her rocking her back and forth. "Hau! A stern voice said to them leaning over to pick up the car. It was the Indians, three very tall elderly men dress in jeans, cowboy boots and fitted button up shirts, but their faces were painted and standing behind them were three women dressed completely in feathers, except for the skirt wrapped around their waist.

Mitchell pulled Sara up from her knees. "Hau!" He said back to them, nodding his head and holding out his hand for them to shake it. "I am Mitchell." He tells them. "This

is my wife Sara and those are our children Tessa and William." He said pointing to the car. The Indians looked over at the car and began to wave and smile. "One missing huh?" The Indian man said holding the car up to his face examining it. "Ah yes," Mitchell tells him. "Jonah he's with them." They all looked up at the house. "Yes, we know where he is, shall we go and get him?" They said walking up the stairway to the house. "I believe you have something that belongs to us, right?" The Indian man said looking at William. "The boy will have to give it to me himself." He tells Mitchell. "Get them and bring them inside." He tells him, Mitchell looked at Sara. "Come honey get Tessa." He tells Sara walking to the car. "Is this going to be safe for them?" Sara asked. "It doesn't matter Sara we have to get Jonah back I don't believe anyone will be harmed." I want my son back, I wasn't planning to bring them into this, but this is what they want, let's just do what they want so that this madness will end Sara come on." He tells her opening the car door. "William get out! He says.

"Dad who are they?" He asked stepping out of the car. "Son these people will help us get Jonah back, they came from the reservation where the drum was to stay." He tells him holding onto his shoulder. "We have to do what they say, now they want you to hand them that drum the way that Sabien handed it to you." He said. "Dad, Sabien had it hidden in his pants, he pulled it from his waist side and handed it to me." He tells his father. "Well son you do exactly that, here you go, put it inside the elastic on your pants so that you don't drop it." He tells him guiding him into the house. When they got inside the Indians were in each corner of the house waving a feathered fan with one hand and smoke coming from the other hand. They chanted at the same time as they went over the walls of the house.

They slowly went around the whole house walking backwards, as soon as William entered with Mitchell, they looked over at him. "Into the center." They all said at the same time. "The center of the house." They tell them, waving the smoke toward all of them. Sara stood in silence holding Tessa on her hip, she looks over at Mitchell, he nods his head yes. She moved forward into the middle of the room with Tessa standing behind Mitchell and William. They stood watching as the begin to mark the walls with the end of the feathers, each wall turned a different color, they made circles with the colors going over them, repeatedly until the circles were as big as the wall. The circles changed

colors with each stroke of the feathers they held in their hands. The colors lit the room around them. The room was so quiet until the colors began to fade into the wall, huge holes begin to open as the colors faded away, when they opened as wide as the walls, they started to hear voices coming from the holes, some whispering, some yelling, some crying. William began to cover his eyes, Tessa cried putting her face into Sara's chest to hide her eyes. Sara held her head close to her. The Indian man turned to William slowly, stepping right in front of him. He put his hand out to ask for the drum, William reached down in his pants pulling the drum from his waist side. The Indian man took the drum from William's hand shaking it all around him, chanting while he did it. He grabbed onto William pulling him toward the wall. "Don't resist come with me." He tells him. "We have to go in to get out, the spirits in here run deeper behind the walls." He tells him looking over at Mitchell. "Wait what do you mean?" Mitchell asked. "We all have to go inside." The man told him waving his hand for them to follow him into the hole. Sara hesitated. "This is the only way to turn this around and to get your son, please follow us in." The man told them. "They will be right behind you all to protect you, don't fear what you can't see." He tells them walking into the wall. They followed him inside the dark hole.

The voices and cries became louder, they could feel the breath of the voices that were whispers as they walked further into the darkness. They followed the shaking of the drum, the lights around the feathers were brightened as they walked further inside. Colors covered the inside of the dark tunnel. "Mommy I'm afraid." William said grabbing her hand. "Don't be afraid son it's okay." Mitchell tells him. "I'm here with you we'll all be fine." He tells him placing his hand on his shoulders walking him inside.

Inside Out

The colored lights covered the walls of the tunnel. The shadow of the feathers followed them in the lights guiding them in. They walked and walked for what seemed like hours. William covered his small ears afraid to hear the screams and whispers. When they reached the end of the tunnel the screams and whispers faded. They could hear water as if they were near a waterfall. It echoed in the tunnel loudly, the Indian man looked at Mitchell. "Hold onto their hands" He told them "Hold them tight and follow me and when I say jump, everyone jumps at the same time." He tells them softly, turning to the others looking up and around them. They held onto one another so tight. "I'm afraid." William said to Sara looking up at her. "Son, no there's no time to be afraid, hold on to me it's okay." She tells him as they get to the edge to jump into the darkness. They all jumped into the darkness following the Indian man and the others. They could hear the echo of the rocks falling hitting the tunnels dark walls. William closed his eyes holding onto Sara's clothing tightly. It seemed that they were flying downward into the darkness of the tunnel. Soon they saw coming toward them in the darkness, a cloud of smoke forming a circle around them. "Hey!" Mitchell yelled out. Only to be given a stern look by the Indian man. All he could see was his eyes in the smoke. "Don't do it, it's okay!" The man yelled out at him. The smoke lifted them like they were being carried by it, in from the darkness to where there was light. Soon they were floating in the smoke down to the gravel and dirt of the tunnel where there was a fire burning in the middle of the closed tunnel.

They begin to see the shadows of many different faces and many different people. Cowboys and Indians alike, it was like they had fallen into another universe. The Indian man warned them not to speak a word as he walked around them in the circle, shifting his arm across them he blew smoke from his funneled horn, at the same time the Indian women shook the tiny drums they held in their right hands dancing around them. William grabbed onto Mitchell with tears in his eyes while Tessa had no fear. She began to reach for all the feathers they wore with all the colors on them. Soon after they danced, and the smoke cleared the Indian man and the cowboy walked over to Mitchell and grabbed him by the arm. They didn't say a word, the Indian man placed the hand drum in his right hand as the cowboy stood holding his left arm, the Indian man guided his hand to the walls of the tunnel. He shook the drum as more spirits began to fill the tunnel. Mitchell was nervous, the cowboy whispered to him. "Send them back now." He said to him. Mitchell looked at him, confused shaking his head. The Indian man took the drum from his hand then placed a black piece of coal into his hand. He took his hand and began to guide him to write with the chalk on the wall circle after circle. The circle went from big and small to big again to small and back. They went down the tunnel all the way to the entrance they came through. The Indian man walked Mitchell back to the fire, sitting down with his back to his with his legs crossed. Mitchell didn't know what to do as they were silent never really speaking a word.

The Indian man began to bellow out of his mouth a chant. His voice echoed throughout the tunnel. They others begin to join him; they shook the drums, dancing around them as the men sat with their backs to them bellowing out the chant for the spirits. Sara held her head down fearing what would come. She held Tessa close to her chest, William sat close, Mitchell closing his eyes tight. Soon the smoke came flowing above the tunnel from the entrance. They could see it flowing slowly as it gets closer to them, it forms a circle in front of the circle where they sat with their backs to the wall, facing the fire. The Indian man lifted his arms and started to shake the drum again. The others joined him shaking the drum as fast as they could, holding it up shaking his arm in a circle. The smoke formed like a tornado, it floated to the top of the tunnel then back down to the bottom, then it was still. Everyone placed their drums down on the ground of the tunnel and laid down, stretching their arms forward when looking up, the smoke began to break into two and formed a small tornado like cloud of smoke, suddenly before them was Jonah, standing next to him was a cowboy holding his shoulder. The Indian man sat up and cleared the pathway for Mitchell and Sara to turn around to see with a nod of his head he smiled at Sara pointing to Jonah, then in a whisper he said to them, "He's safe come with me." He said to Sara reaching his hand out to her. She grabbed onto his hand standing to her feet. They walked over to the cowboy. Sara wanted to grab Jonah, but she knew this wasn't the time, the cowboy's spirit was very protective of him he looked very anger as they walked toward them. In the light from the fire, you could see the shadows of the Indian man's feathers waving. Tessa sat staring at all the feathers while Mitchell nervously waited to see what would happen with Jonah.

"Sara put your hand there." He said taking her hands, placing them onto Jonah's shoulders. "Don't move them. Sara was very scared; she didn't know what the cowboy would do he looked very angry that she was standing there. Tears rolled from Sara's eyes as she wanted to grab onto

Jonah and run with him, but she knew she must abide by what the Indian man was advising her to do, she stood still there holding onto Jonah's shoulders as he told her. The Indian man whispered to her. "Move with him to your right near the wall quickly." He tells her looking at the wall. "Now!" He tells her. He took the drum from the ground as Sara ran over to the wall. "Stand with your back there." The Indian man told her. He began to shake the drum all around the spirit of the cowboy. The cowboy began to fade from the bottom of his feet to the top of his head, he formed back into the smoke cloud that he appeared in. The Indian man walked over to her and Jonah. "Hold onto him." He said covering them from the sight of the smoke he guided them back over to the circle where he placed Jonah into the middle of the circle. "Your boy is a spirit finder, they cling to him because his soul is open of no fear of them, we have to protect him from another one latching onto him before we send them back." He told them sitting back on the ground with his back to Mitchells, shaking the drum he began to bellow out of his mouth the loudest howl as if he was a wolf, the others began to howl along with him. The smoke covered the tunnel then up to the top of the tunnel it went, as they chanted and sang and howled. The smoke moved as if it was dancing with the songs they sang.

They all went silent shaking the drums over their heads in silence. They all dropped the drums and turned around forming a tight circle around Sara, Mitchell and the kids with Jonah in the middle. The Indian man handed William the drum guiding his hand to shake it. The smoke was still over them it began to move slowly down toward the fire, then suddenly it dropped down into the fire. Soul after soul went into the fire with the smoke. Some of them went quietly, some of them made loud angry sounds. Jonah covered his eyes every time he heard them make an angry sound. Soon the darkness hit the tunnel. They couldn't see at all. They held onto each other afraid to say a word. Mitchell rubbed his hand over Sara's back, she held onto Jonah's small hands as Tessa clutched onto William, trying to see through the darkness. The Indian man stood up from the circle along with the others. "This way!" He said pulling on Mitchell's shirt. "Grab onto your wife and children, stay together don't move to fast!" He said guiding them back through the darkness, toward the entrance where they came from. The Indian man stopped them. The others formed a circle around them. "This is the important part." he tells them standing behind them. "Hold hands, now lift them all together up over your heads and keep them there even the baby, hurry!" He tells them as they felt like something was pulling them together, like a tight rope but they couldn't see anything. They stood there holding their hands up to the tunnel they were pulled close together, it felt tighter and tighter. Mitchell almost yelled out as it seemed to tighten up more, he was still with Jonah in the middle. The Indian began to chant. They felt like they were being lifted from their feet, then suddenly they were upside down, then a hard push took them downward into more darkness. Sara couldn't help herself she began to scream. They were falling, the wind blew in their ears like a whistle, they were going so fast downward.

Suddenly they dropped onto a soft surface with their eyes closed tight not knowing what to expect. Mitchell grabbed onto Sara's wais.t "Baby are you okay?" He asked her. "I am." She responded, "The kids?" He asked. Still with his eyes closed. "Mommy, daddy we're safe!" Tessa said in a whisper, touching Mitchell's face with her small hands. "Daddy open your eyes! Open them mommy we're safe." Tessa said, Mitchell and Sara opened their eyes. They were on the bed in their room. The bed was covered in colorful feathers, they looked at one another. "Is it over?" Mitchell asked Sara. "I think it's over Sara said to him getting off the bed, holding onto Jonah. "Baby are you okay?" She asked Jonah. "I am mommy, I'm okay." He tells her. "And look who's talking to us now!" He said pointing at Tessa. "Yes, you spoke sweetie. Mitchell said to her grabbing her from the feathers. William stood to his feet from the bed. "Dad is it over? He asked him. "Son, I don't know, I hope so." They heard a knock on the door "Come on." Mitchell said carrying Tessa to the door. "Is it safe honey?" Sara asked, Mitchell shrugged his shoulders "We shall see." He said turning the nob to the door, opening it slowly peeking out. They all walked together toward the stairwell of the house, looking all around the hallway assuring themselves that no other spirit would show up, Mitchell went first down the stairs.

Normal

When they got downstairs Mitchell check the peephole on the door before opening it. Standing outside the door was the Indian man and the three other Indians he'd come with; he opened the door. "Hi!" He said excited. The Indian man nodded his head to him and crossed his left hand to his chest stretching his hand out to him with his hand closed. His fingers were covered in jewels. Mitchell reached his hand out. "You keep this to cover your house and your family, they are gone." He tells Mitchell smiling. Mitchell smiles back. "Thank you so much." He says to him shutting the door. Mitchell turned to Sara. "It's done baby, we're good now." He says, grabbing her, holding her close to him, looking at the children sitting down on the couch looking out of the window. "Who was that dad?" Jonah asked. Mitchell and Sara looked at one another shocked. "Just a friend." Mitchell tells him walking toward him. The kids seemed to have forgotten everything they had gone through when they moved in. The family ate dinner that night at the table. They heard the neighbors outside in the back playing with their children in the playground. They ate in silence. Sara was still in a bit of a shock but said nothing to Mitchell about the ordeal as she knew the children had no memories of what they'd been through. Jonah was a little strange watching the kids playing from his seat at the dinner table. He chewed on his bread very slowly. "You alright?" Mitchell asked him. He nodded his head back and forth slowly. "You sure?" Mitchell asked. He nods again this time placing his bread on the plate, turning his back all the way toward the slide in door.

"Can I play outside with the kid's dad?" He asked. Mitchell looked at Sara, she shrugged her shoulders. "I

don't see why not." She told him. "So, you're not hungry?"
Mitchell asked him. "I ate a little." Jonah told him standing
from the table. "William, would you like to come out with
me, we can play football or four squares?" He asked.
William shook his head quickly no. "Sure?" Jonah asked
again. "Yes, I'm sure." William tells him getting up from
the table walking to the bathroom to wash his hands. "I'm
done mom, thank you." He says walking into the bathroom.
He shuts the door of the bathroom. Sara and Mitchell
looked at one another concerned. "Did he seem okay to
you?" Mitchell asked her. "I don't know Mitchell they've
been through so much; they may not remember but they
seem so tired, look at Jonah." Sara said looking out at
Jonah as he tossed the ball back and forth from one hand to
another slowly. "Ah I think they just need to rest." Mitchell
tells her. "You're right, I'm sure that's all it is." Sara said
clearing the table. Tessa sat quietly still nibbling at her
dinner, William came out of the bathroom to the living
room couch where Mitchell was sitting having his coffee
after dinner. "You, okay?" Mitchell asked him once more.
"I am dad just tired." He tells him sitting down next to him,
grabbing the pillow from the couch clutching it to his chest,
leaning over with his head to the floor. Mitchell looked
back at Sara and Tessa. "I'm going to make a call to the
ship baby I'll be upstairs" Mitchell tells her getting up from
the couch "Okay we'll be up soon." She says to him
working on the dishes, cleaning all around Tessa as she still
nibbled at her food. Jonah came back into the house. He
went over to the table standing next to Tessa, he began to
take a carrot from her plate eating it. "Mommy where did
those feathers come from on the bed?" He asked her. Sara
put the dish towel down on the table she went over to him,
not knowing what to tell him as he'd forgotten. She sat

down looking him in his eyes. "Son those were a gift from a time we had." She tells him. "A gift?" He asked. "Yes, a gift of for a new beginning." She tells him, she gave him a very big hug holding him close to her. "Come on son let's get your sister cleaned up." She said grabbing the wipes from the shelf, she began wiping Tessa's hand and face. "Messy baby!" She happily sang to Tessa as she cleaned her off, Jonah would grab the dirty wipes tossing them into the garbage can. They all headed up to bed when they were done. Sara looked back down at the kitchen thankful for the peace that now surrounded the house as the kids walked ahead of her to the stairwell. When they reached the top of the stairwell, there standing before them was a very tall Indian man wearing a feathered blue skirt, no shirt, feathers around his ankles and his head, barefoot. Sara was startled, she stopped in her tracks, pulling the children back. The Indian man shouted out, howling out at them with wind so forceful it pushed them down the stairwell onto their backs. When they looked up there was a cloud of red smoke flowing over their heads. Their calm was gone.

The End

About the Author

K.C McGee born March 7th, 1972, to Mr. & Mrs. Ernest and Ruth Love. While her journey has been altered throughout her life, she pressed forward raising her nine children, she pursued her career as a Novelist while working and studying Behavioral Health at UCSD, she is now on her journey to becoming a well-known novelist captivating reader with her five-book series and more, building her legacy for her children. Today she is a published Author pursuing her dream.

www.ingramcontent.com/pod-product-compliance
Lightning Source LLC
Chambersburg PA
CBHW051109030726
47504CB00006B/1856